FOR A *Rogue*

The Honorable Rogues®, Book Two

COLLETTE CAMERON

Blue Rose Romance®
Portland, Oregon

Sweet-to-Spicy Timeless Romance®

A BRIDE FOR A ROGUE
The Honorable Rogues®, Book Two
Copyright © 2015 Collette Cameron
Cover Design by: Darlene Albert

This book is a work of fiction. Names, characters, places, and incidents are the product of the author's imagination or are used fictitiously. Any resemblance to actual events, locales, or persons, living or dead, is coincidental.

All rights reserved under International and Pan-American Copyright Conventions. By downloading or purchasing a print copy of this book, you have been granted the non-exclusive, non-transferable right to access and read the text of this book. No part of this text may be reproduced, transmitted, downloaded, decompiled, reverse engineered, or stored in or introduced into any information storage and retrieval system, in any form or by any means, whether electronic or mechanical, now known or hereinafter invented without the express written permission of copyright owner.

Attn: Permissions Coordinator
Blue Rose Romance®
8420 N Ivanhoe # 83054
Portland, Oregon 97203

eBook ISBN: 9781954307384
Paperback ISBN: 9781954307391
www.collettecameron.com

"I want to kiss you."

Not more than an inch separated their lips. "Yes." She dared not breathe, having waited for this moment for so long, nothing must disturb the magic. "You're sure?" Nostrils flared, his hot gaze fastened on her lips. Ever the gentleman, Falcon paused and lifted his desire-laden eyes to hers. He brushed her lower lip with his thumb again. "You want me to continue?" Woman's intuition told her he asked for much more than a kiss or two. Ivonne smiled, past caring if he knew the secret she'd long nurtured in her soul.

"I've waited a lifetime to kiss you."

"Beautiful chemistry...
You'll cheer forthese star-crossed lovers."
Christi Gladwell USA Today Bestselling Author

Other Collette Cameron Books

The Honorable Rogues®
A Kiss for a Rogue
A Bride for a Rogue
A Rogue's Scandalous Wish
To Capture a Rogue's Heart
The Rogue and the Wallflower
A Rose for a Rogue

Check out Collette's Other Series
Castle Brides
Highland Heather Romancing a Scot
Daughters of Desire (Scandalous Ladies)
The Blue Rose Regency Romances:
The Culpepper Misses
Seductive Scoundrels
Heart of a Scot

Collections
Lords in Love
The Honorable Rogues® Books 1-3
The Honorable Rogues® Books 4-6
Seductive Scoundrels Series Books 1-3
Seductive Scoundrels Series Books 4-6
The Blue Rose Regency Romances-
The Culpepper Misses Series 1-2

A Bride for a Rogue is for you, Grandma Cameron.

I only wished you'd lived to read my books.

Who knew I had so many stories waiting to be told?

Acknowledgements

As always, I owe a huge thanks to my critique partners and beta readers. Your honesty, insight, and suggestions have been invaluable to me.

To my cover artist, Darlene Albert, editor, Danielle Fine, and virtual assistant, Cindy Jackson, mega hugs!

And to my wonderful VIP reader group, Collette's Chéris. Thank you, darlings, for all you do!

xoxo

Collette

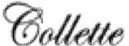

London, England
Late May, 1818

"There you are, Miss Wimpleton."

Ivonne Wimpleton whipped her gaze to Captain Melvin Kirkpatrick. Groaning in frustration, she snapped her fan closed, prepared to use the frilly accessory to give him a good poke or two, if necessary.

Fiend seize it. What is he doing here?

He must have arrived after she ventured outdoors.

She'd specifically asked Mother not to invite him tonight. Somehow, the boor had finagled an invitation to accompany another guest. Ivonne had hoped he'd finally sailed for Africa and wouldn't impose his unwelcome presence on her for six blessed months or more.

He staggered toward her secluded bench on the side terrace, a drunken smile skewing his mouth.

She shot to her feet, searching for a means to avoid him. The only possibility lay in the narrow stairway descending to the manicured garden where an occasional colored lantern glowed. Ivonne strode toward her salvation at a near run.

Captain Kirkpatrick caught her arm and pinned her against the balustrade with his great weight. Her fan fell, clattering to the flagstone.

Straining against him, Ivonne fought to breathe and gagged. Did the man ever bathe?

"What audacity. Unhand me, sir!"

He shook his head. Excitement glimmered in his glassy eyes. "I think not. You've played the reluctant miss long enough. It's time you tasted what our married life will be like."

"Are you dicked in the nob?" Though no match for his strength, Ivonne still fought to break free. As she struggled, her hair pins came loose and scattered onto the stones. "I. Am. Not. Marrying. You."

He tightened his clasp, and she winced as he held her arms in a bruising grip.

"I prefer blondes with blue eyes, but I cannot complain about your curves." Leering at her bosom, Captain Kirkpatrick licked his lips. He pawed her breast with one beefy hand as his other gripped her head in an attempt to steal a kiss.

His foul breath assailed Ivonne, sending her stomach pitching at the stench of strong spirits and onions. Intent on screaming like a banshee, she opened her mouth and sucked in a huge breath.

A chortling foursome of gentlemen burst through the French windows onto the other side of the terrace. Their sudden appearance rescued her from the captain's lewd groping. Panting heavily, his bushy red eyebrows scrunched together, he released her and scowled at her brother, Allen, Lords Sethwick and Luxmoore, and the Duke of Harcourt.

A pity the new arrivals weren't her twin cousins, Edwina and Edward. They would come to her aid and not breathe a word of the untoward situation. However, if Allen spied her in Captain Kirkpatrick's company, there would be the devil to pay.

Ivonne tried to blend into the manor's shadow, but the sea captain's stout form obstructed her. Her brother had warned the widower away from her once already. If he suspected the captain dared lay a hand on her, Allen would call him out. A dab hand at pistols—all firearms, for that matter—Captain Kirkpatrick might wound, or, heaven forbid, kill dear Allen.

She shuddered. It must not come to that. She peeked at the captain from beneath her lashes. More than a trifle disguised, his drunken focus remained on the other men. Ivonne seized the moment. Without hesitation, she kneed him in the ballocks with her good leg and gave him a mighty shove.

Bent double and growling in fury, he stumbled backward, clutching his groin.

Ignoring his gasps of pain and vile curses, she edged away. With one eye on the laughing quartet, she crept down the stairs. Once out of their view, she flew across the lawn as rapidly as her injured leg would allow. She'd broken the limb in two places in a riding accident three years ago. The leg pained her on occasion, and she endured a permanent, though slight, limp made worse by overexertion.

She darted behind a tall rose-covered trellis. In her haste, the ball gown's black net overskirt caught on a thorn-laden cane. Breathing labored and leg throbbing, she halted just inside the alcove and gave the skirt a gentle tug.

Dash it all. Stuck fast.

She sent a frantic glance along the footpath.

A twig snapped. Had Captain Kirkpatrick followed her?

A jolt of fright raised the hairs on her arms and stole her breath. Did she dare step outside the arbor and release the material? Would he see her if she did? She couldn't move farther into the enclosure, though if she remained here, she risked almost certain discovery.

A sleepy dove cooed from somewhere in the garden's trees. The night's festivities had no doubt disturbed its slumber.

Ivonne peered through the lattice slats.

Where was he?

With her forefinger, she nudged a couple of leaves aside. Her white gloves stood out, a stark contrast against the plants. Oh, to have the mythical mantel of Arthur in Cornwall and be invisible.

A soft wind wafted through her hiding place and rustled the leaves overhead. Several spun lazily to the ground. Guests' laughter and the lilting strains of the orchestra floated through the beveled French windows and carried to her on the mild breeze.

What possessed her to give into the impulse to venture outside alone and catch some air?

Because you dislike balls, gentlemen treating you as if you're beneath their touch, and all the pretentious nastiness that's generally present when the denizens of High Society gather.

Though only May, the crush of the crowd inside the mansion caused the temperature to rise uncomfortably. The heat, mixed with cloying perfumes, less-than-fresh clothing, the aroma of dozens of beeswax candles, and the occasional unbathed body, made her head ache and stomach queasy.

She'd sought a secluded niche on the side terrace

to recover. Unfortunately, Captain Kirkpatrick, deep in his cups, found her there. Much like the shaggy bull he resembled, he'd stalked her at every social gathering.

A more off-putting man she'd never met.

Ivonne turned sideways and hoped the vines' thick cover concealed her. If fear had a scent, the captain's bulbous nose would lead him straight to her. Heavy footfalls crunched upon the gravel not more than a yard away. She closed her eyes as her heart lurched to her throat. Thank God she hadn't tried to detach her gown. He'd have been on her like dense winter fog on the River Thames.

"Miss Wimpleton, you saucy minx, where are you?"

A low, suggestive chuckle followed. "I do like a spirited gel in my bed. I do, indeed."

Ivonne's eyes popped open. Captain Kirkpatrick's gloating singsong whisper sent a shiver of loathing the length of her spine. She bit her lower lip, afraid to exhale lest he detect her presence.

He advanced another foot, pausing before the lattice.

She clenched her jaw and shut her eyes.

He stood so close, the noxious mixture of his dinner, pungent cologne, and sweat assaulted her nose. Hot bile rose to her throat, and she swallowed against the burning. Her nose twitched. Flaring her nostrils, she fought to suppress a sneeze.

If he discovered her hidden within the nook, there'd be no escaping the man's amorous attentions. He might claim to prefer blondes, but he'd become bolder each time she encountered him. Given the opportunity, God alone knew what the foxed knave might try in this private bower. Look what he'd attempted on the veranda in full view of anyone who might have come along.

Holding her breath, she pursed her lips.

Do not sneeze.

The captain planted his hands on his ample hips and scanned the shrubberies. He turned in a slow circle. The straining gold buttons of his black tailcoat gleamed in the moonbeams bathing the path. He withdrew a silver flask from his pocket, and after a furtive glance around, took a couple of healthy gulps.

"Where are you? Come out, my sweet." He belched and returned the flask to his pocket. "No need to be coy. I have something of importance to ask you."

Precisely why Ivonne huddled like a timid mouse amongst the foliage outside her parents' mansion. In the past two months, he'd asked the same question thrice before. Her firm "No" each time hadn't deterred him in the least. In fact, her reluctance appeared to make the stocky widower more determined to win her hand.

Grimacing and cautious to keep her gown from rustling, she shifted her weight to her good leg.

Ah, much better.

Wisteria and salmon-colored climbing roses concealed the garden nook. Her favorite hideaway, normally, she would have relished the fragrant air surrounding her. Tonight, however, she could only be grateful the roses' scent masked her perfume and hadn't produced a fit of sneezing.

Ivonne swallowed against the tickle teasing her throat. If only she dared pinch her nostrils. She mustn't. Her gloves against the verdant leaves might give her away. Yearning to slip into one of the nook's inky corners, she yanked her skirt again. The fabric didn't budge.

Captain Kirkpatrick swung his dark gaze to the trellis.

P etrified, Ivonne mouthed a silent prayer.
Dear God, don't let him find me.

The distant glow pouring from the manor's open doors bathed the captain in muted light. Kirkpatrick turned his head from side to side, a perplexed frown on his broad face.

"Where'd the chit get to?"

She nearly wept with relief. He hadn't discovered her after all.

Muttering a vulgar curse, he scowled at the couple strolling along the path in his direction.

Bless, Edmund and Edwina. Their presence in the garden wasn't accidental. They must have been looking for her and followed Captain Kirkpatrick. They wouldn't leave her to his mercy.

"Mr. Linville. Miss Linville." He offered the briefest of bows.

Edwina favored him with a tight-lipped smile. "It's a splendid evening for a turn about the gardens. The honeysuckle there," she pointed in the opposite direction of the alcove, "smells divine, does it not, Captain?"

"Er, indeed." He didn't spare the fragrant vine a glimpse. He peered behind them. "You haven't seen Miss Wimpleton, have you?"

Edmund canted his blond head. "Why no, not since I asked her to dance."

"She danced with you? She told me she doesn't dance." Scowling, Captain Kirkpatrick scratched his buttocks.

Staring pointedly at his indecorous behavior, Edwina raised a fair eyebrow.

"No, she doesn't dance anymore, but I still like to make the offer." Edmund flashed one of his engaging smiles. "Ivonne wanted to try her hand at cards tonight. Claimed she felt lucky."

Cards bored Ivonne as much as French lessons or gossip of Prinny, yet she would play the entire night if she didn't have to dance. Never nimble on her feet, with a lame leg, she'd become even less so. A blindfolded elephant in half-boots possessed more grace than she.

Creating a spectacle before two hundred guests again was unthinkable. She had done so once before and found herself plopped upon her derriere, her gown mid-thigh, exposing her legs for all to see. She no longer danced, and gentlemen rarely asked her to. Nonetheless, Edmund always made a token request at those gatherings that included dancing as part of the evening's entertainment.

Her nostrils tingled in warning. Eyes watering, she pressed her teeth together.

Don't sneeze. Don't sneeze.

Do. Not. Sneeze, Ivonne Georgina Augusta Wimpleton.

"Cards, eh?" Captain Kirkpatrick rubbed his chins. "She was taking the air on the terrace a few minutes ago. I'm positive I saw her wandering along this path."

Lying buffoon.

"Oh, I'm sure you're mistaken, Captain." Edwina's voice acquired a harsh edge. "Ivonne might be set upon by an uncouth, *inebriated* lout if she strolled about alone. Lord and Lady Wimpleton would be most displeased if such a thing befell their daughter."

Brava, Edwina.

"Why don't you accompany us inside?" Edmund turned his sister in the direction of the house. "We'll look for Ivonne together."

Ivonne smiled. Her cousins would have the widower examining every unused, cobwebby cranny in the manor. She held her breath against another potential sneeze. Something else must be in bloom. Roses didn't cause her this distress.

The captain shook his oversized, red-haired head. "I'll be along in a moment or two. It's too hot in the house, and I need a few moments more to cool off."

He removed his handkerchief from his coat pocket.

In the faint light, Ivonne detected thick beads of sweat glistening on his mottled features. He did rather resemble a great lathered ox. Truth to tell, everything about the man shouted brutish beast, from his thick-set build, bullish shoulders, and wide face, to his bulging round brown eyes, clomping walk, and gruff, deep-toned voice.

After wiping his damp face, he returned the sopped cloth to his pocket.

Ivonne swore Edwina slid a sidelong glance in the trellis's direction. No surprise there. Her dearest friends, the twins had spent many hours sequestered in this sanctuary with her.

Another sneeze threatened. Ivonne wriggled her nose and twisted her lips, fighting the urge. Was there anything as annoying as trying *not* to sneeze?

Oh, do go along, Captain, will you?

How much longer could she keep stifling her sneezes?

"Captain, I do believe Lady Wimpleton has a delicious iced punch for the gentlemen. A cup or two of the bracing beverage ought to refresh you." Edwina linked her arm with Captain Kirkpatrick's.

Bold as brass was Edwina. Given the man's malodorous form, she was stoic as an undertaker, as well.

"S'pose it would at that." He allowed himself to be led away. Before rounding the footpath's bend, he glanced over his shoulder. His intense gaze lingered on Ivonne's hiding place.

Could he see her?

She retreated and gave her gown a fierce yank. The fabric tore free. The force rattled the lattice, bathing her in a lush shower of petals and leaves. Mouth closed, she sneezed into her hand. A strangled snort emerged.

"What was that?" Captain Kirkpatrick spun around. His gait unsteady, he pounded toward the arbor.

Edwina and Edmund tore along behind him.

Ivonne stepped backward.

Once. Twice. Three times. And bumped into a figure obscured at the rear of the arbor. She shrieked and lunged to flee the alcove.

Firm arms encircled her.

"Hello, Ivy," a familiar male voice whispered in her ear.

3

Chancey Faulkenhurst inhaled Ivy's perfume, relishing the unexpected gift of holding her in his arms. He wanted to kiss her, drink in her essence, water his parched soul with her sweetness.

God, he'd missed her.

"Falcon?" Wonder in her voice, she turned and touched his face. "Is it really you?"

He released a low chuckle. "Indeed, Ivy, it is."

Her nickname slipped from his tongue as if, instead of six long years, he'd seen her yesterday. He'd dubbed her Ivy a score ago—whenever he and Allen came up from school on holiday, she'd clung to them as tenaciously as an ivy vine—and the pet name stuck.

She'd been infuriated and began calling him Falcon instead of Chance as his friends did. He'd rather liked the nickname until her brother started tossing it about. Now, most of Chance's intimate friends addressed him as Falcon.

He wished he could see her features clearly. The fragmented moonbeams revealed little more than ivory skin, dark plum lips, and shiny eyes.

Ivy's gaze sank to his cheek. Her glorious eyes widened, and her breath caught. She brushed a hesitant finger across the scar. "What's this? You've been hurt? Why did no one tell me?"

The puckered inch-long streak was the least of his wounds. Nonetheless, her concern warmed his cynical heart. A heart he'd long ago given to her, though she mustn't know.

He wasn't free to woo her.

"Shh. It's naught." Chance caught her hand with his good one. He pressed her palm to his chest, the only affection he dared show. "I take it you're hiding from that half-sprung brute?"

He tilted his head in the direction of the approaching footsteps. Ivy probably couldn't see the movement.

"That obnoxious fellow. Has he been both—"

Kirkpatrick plowed into the arbor, sending another cascade of leaves and petals down upon them. Wheezing, he swung his head back and forth like an enraged bull.

"What goes on here?" he bellowed, sounding much like the creature he resembled.

The fair-haired duo plunged into the bower's other side.

Stifling a snicker, Chance grinned. They reminded him of a pair of fierce pugs ready to take on a bull mastiff. Kirkpatrick didn't stand a tick's chance in hot oil against Ivy's two determined protectors.

The captain drew himself up, his large frame blocking what light managed to penetrate the slats. "Miss Wimpleton, as my future wife, I demand to know. What are you doing in the arms of this man?"

Chest heaving, he flicked his thick fingers contemptuously at Chance.

"Your future wife?" Ivy stiffened and whirled to face the captain. "Have you taken leave of your senses?"

She trembled. In outrage or fear? Both, perhaps.

Ivy made no attempt to step away from Chance, and he allowed himself a pleased smile.

Kirkpatrick scowled and narrowed his eyes to infuriated slits when Chance didn't release her.

He firmed his embrace a fraction, silently challenging the ox.

The other pair stared at his arms encircling her. As one, they raised questioning gazes to his.

Were they prone to nattering? Best not to give them more juicy tidbits to spread about. He reluctantly withdrew his arms, but rested one hand on the small of Ivy's back, as much to satisfy his need to touch her after all this time as to lend her comfort and support.

She wrapped her arms around her middle and edged a step closer to him. Odd, she'd never been one to retreat from a challenge. She did fear the man. That warranted further investigation.

Chance leveled the captain a furious glare.

Voice raspy, she said, "Captain Kirkpatrick, I have told you three times already. I *do not* want to marry you. I *shall not* marry you."

"Three times? Persistent bloke, isn't he?" Chance made no attempt to keep the mockery from his voice.

The twins—Edwina and Edmund Linville, if Chance recalled correctly—laughed.

Giggling, Miss Linville managed, "And those were just the formal proposals. There were at least another half dozen written ones."

"Along with some ... ah ... *creative* poetry scribbled on the reverse of calling cards jammed into bouquets." Edmund offered those morsels, seemingly unaffected by the hostile glower Kirkpatrick leveled at him. In fact, brazen as a doxy on a Saturday night, the plucky fellow winked at the captain. "Delivered every Monday and Thursday, I believe."

Chance took the captain's measure. "You don't say. Perhaps persistent is the wrong word. I'd suggest obsessed might be more apt."

Ivy nodded, the silky hairs on her crown, tickling his chin.

A good portion of the russet strands tumbled about her shoulders. How had her hair come to be in such disarray? Had that sot dared to touch her? Through a haze of ire, Chance tamped down his desire to rearrange the seaman's beefy features. Instead, he concentrated on Ivy's rounded behind pressing into his groin. All sorts of distracting images soared forth as his manhood twitched in approval.

"What say you, Ivy? Have the captain's attentions become bothersome?" Chance pressed her spine gently.

Her focus on Kirkpatrick, she tilted her head. "Yes, Mr. Faulkenhurst, though I've asked him to leave off several times."

She smelled divine, a mixture of spring rain and iris. Chance enjoyed a pleasant view of the valley between the creamy bosoms swelling above her gown's neckline. She made no attempt to put a respectable distance between them.

Then again, she regarded him as a harmless older brother. One of the reasons, at three and twenty, he'd petitioned for a transfer to India to support the East India troops. A harmless older brother didn't harbor the sensual fantasies she elicited in him or want to step closer to enjoy her womanly curves more fully.

Though a commissioned lieutenant in His Majesty's Regiments, as a second son of an earl, he had nothing to offer a viscount's daughter except a hundred or so sheep and a long-neglected estate in Cheshire his mother bequeathed him. Did Foxbrooke Cottage even remain standing? When he'd last heard, the rundown house wasn't fit for habitants other than vermin and insects.

He couldn't claim an officer's income anymore either. Naturally, he'd sell his commission, but at less than twelve hundred pounds, the monies wouldn't begin to restore Foxbrooke, let alone support Ivy in the manner she was accustomed to.

He could seek a position as a steward or a secretary with one of his titled friends. However, with a hand short two fingers, writing presented a challenge. Would offers of employment be prompted by pity rather than genuine need? Heaven forbid. He continued to practice writing with his right hand but made slower progress than he wished. And truth to tell, even if gainfully employed, he'd not be worthy of Ivy.

The damnable agreement Father contrived with his

crony, Lord Lambert, while Chance fought in India, presented a rather troublesome complication too. For a hefty marriage settlement, his sire pledged Chance would marry Lambert's widowed daughter, Cornelia Washburn, when he returned to England.

Eight years his senior, if Chance's memory served correctly, she possessed a termagant's temperament and had one eye that was wont to look off sideways.

He adjusted his injured arm, and white pain vibrated to his shoulder. The wound hadn't completely healed. The optimistic surgeon who'd repaired the limb assured Chance he'd get *most* of the use of his arm back, though the same couldn't be guaranteed of his hand.

Astute fellow. One could assume the man of medicine had never known a human to regrow fingers.

The twins advanced further into the arbor, their hostile gazes raking the fuming captain.

Linville brushed a strand of hair off his forehead and met Chance's gaze. "Allen told the captain to desist in his addresses, yet he continues to pursue Ivonne."

"I've given him no cause whatsoever to encourage his attentions." Ivy glanced at Chance, desperation in her eyes. "I've taken to avoiding him at every turn."

She held her head high, although he detected the tremor in her voice. Kirkpatrick terrified her. Chance reached for his sword, but his hand met air. The blade no longer hung by his side. He'd like nothing better than to run the captain—in his cups or not—through for tormenting Ivy.

"Why don't you leave off? Miss Wimpleton has made it clear she doesn't return your regard." Chance turned his blandest stare on the seaman.

Kirkpatrick grunted and waved his hand. "It's not like she has a multitude of other offers. I'm the only man of means who's shown any interest in her this season."

Bloody bastard.

Ivy drew in a swift breath and stiffened. "My offers are none of your concern."

"Have you set your sights on one of those pretty pocket-to-let milksops whose only interest in you is your sizable settlement?" He wiped his mouth with the back of his hand and blundered on. "Once wed, they'll retire you to a countryside hovel and not look upon you again."

She snorted. "Don't pretend you're not as interested in my portion, Captain. Though we both know it's Garnkirk House you covet."

"Garnkirk House?" Chance wasn't familiar with the place.

She gave a sharp nod. "An estate—mine upon my marriage—near the Scottish border."

Kirkpatrick puffed out his barrel chest. "I, at least, am prepared to overlook your limp—"

Limp? What limp?

"—and unremarkable appearance to keep you at my side." A self-satisfied smile bent the captain's mouth. He ogled Ivy's breasts, clearly finding her far more appealing than he admitted.

Damn him to hell.

Fury gripped Chance. He didn't care if excess drink had emboldened Kirkpatrick, the churl deserved a sound throttling.

Was the lackwit blind? Ivy was exquisite. At least

the woman-child Chance had left behind had been.

The light in the arbor only hinted at her current loveliness, though he had no doubt she'd developed into a rare beauty. Nothing ostentatious like a diamond or ruby, but rather a pearl or opal, stunning in its innocent simplicity. The delightful creature he'd held in his arms moments ago had been perfectly rounded in the right places too. The recollection sparked a predictable and uncomfortable response from his manhood.

Chance itched to plant Kirkpatrick a facer. Breaking the knuckles of his remaining decent hand would be worth it. Only years of soldiering lent him the self-control he required to warn the captain with words rather than pummel the bounder with fists.

Sometimes, being a gentleman was a blasted bore.

"You step beyond the mark, Captain. Way beyond." Chance curved his fingers around Ivy's slender waist.

She shivered and scooted nearer to him.

Muted voices sounded outside. He cocked his head. Allen and his chums? Chance smiled to himself. Yes. This ought to get very interesting.

He scratched his nose. "Pray tell me, Kirkpatrick, why, in all that's holy, would Miss Wimpleton marry you after you've publically insulted her?"

Let the seadog rant on. He wouldn't be allowed anywhere near the upper salons or *haut ton* gatherings once Harcourt and the others gave the captain the cut direct.

Kirkpatrick pointed a stubby finger at her. "She ought to be grateful I'd consider wedding a chit almost on the shelf."

Ivy and Miss Linville gasped in mutual indignation.

"You misbegotten cur!" Hands fisted, Linville made to confront the captain.

Chance's hand to the young buck's shoulder stayed him. "Don't. The sot's burying himself, good and deep. He's neck high in horse manure. A couple more words and the dolt will be choking on the filth."

Captain Kirkpatrick narrowed his eyes, scowling at Ivy.

"Don't tell me you intend to accept decrepit Lord Walsingham or doddering Lord Craythorn? Both are sixty if they're a day." He lifted his nose and raked her from toe to top, his censure obvious. "You told me you adored children. Neither of those codgers could get a child on you a decade ago, let alone now."

More gasps followed his crass statement.

God rot the bloody bugger.

Smirking, Kirkpatrick patted his chest. "I assure you, I'd have you expecting in a blink."

Ivy made an inarticulate sound and swayed.

Chance steadied her, clenching his jaw against the oaths surging to his tongue. He ached to call the oaf out. Wisdom warned him that to do so meant certain death. His fighting arm was useless. Frustration and impotent rage seized him. He couldn't protect Ivy the way she deserved.

Through half-closed eyes, he observed her.

Profile to Chance, she stared at Kirkpatrick. An almost undiscernible curling of her upper lip hinted at the repugnance she attempted to conceal. Her rapidly rising and falling breasts revealed her agitation.

Did she think Chance a coward for not confronting the captain? The idea stung sharper than his wounded arm. By God, he'd die to protect her, but he wasn't a dullard. Cunning and shrewdness must be his weapons of choice.

Kirkpatrick, wrapped in his own self-importance, seemed oblivious to her contempt. "Why, I have five strapping boys already."

"Ill-mannered bratlings you mean." Miss Linville jutted her chin skyward and glared at him. "Horrid little fat beasts."

"Indeed they are." By way of explanation, Edmund added, "We came upon them in Green Park last week. The older two chased a terrified dog, the middle two threw pebbles at passersby, and the toddler had dropped his drawers in full view of everyone to relieve himself on a tree."

Chance choked on a guffaw.

God's toenails.

Ivy *must* be spared such horror.

She stalked to Captain Kirkpatrick and slanted her head to meet his gaze square on.

There was the feisty girl Chance remembered.

"You pretentious buffoon. You think I'm so desperate to avoid spinsterhood, I'd accept the likes of you?" Her voice quivered and raised an octave with her last few clipped words.

Spinsterhood?

Ivy couldn't be more than, what? One or two and twenty? Hardly old maid material.

Three tall forms shadowed the trellis outside. Ah, the reinforcements had arrived.

Chance stepped beside Ivy. "If you have a lick of sense, Kirkpatrick, you'll leave now."

The captain swaggered further into the bower. "Or what? You'll make me? Ivonne is all but betrothed to me. Her father has as much as promised me her hand."

"No. He has not." Ivy clasped a hand across her mouth, backing away and shaking her head. "He wouldn't."

"That's a brazen lie!"

"How dare you address her by her first name?"

The Linville twins' voices rang out in unison.

Chance allowed a slow grin to tilt his lips. "Impossible."

Ivy peered at him, curiosity in her gaze.

He took her quaking hand in his, careful to keep his disfigured fingers tucked inside his coat. "You see, Kirkpatrick, Ivy is already promised to ... another."

4

Promised?

Ivonne angled her head. She'd misheard. Her nerves and this hullabaloo with Captain Kirkpatrick had her hearing ridiculous things.

Silly goosecap.

Falcon hadn't announced she was pledged to another. Had he?

She tried to read his expression in the muted light. What was he about? Trying to protect her? He almost sounded jealous.

The notion sent a delicious spark to her middle, and the warmth spread to other unmentionable parts in a most curious fashion. She shifted to alleviate the peculiar sensation.

He didn't know that Captain Kirkpatrick wouldn't rest until he unearthed her phantom intended. The widower wanted Garnkirk House. The one hundred eighty acre estate boasted prime hunting and fishing lands. The captain's obsession with his hobbies bordered on unhealthy.

Falcon's long absence from the *ton* had kept him ignorant of Kirkpatrick's reputation. The wealthy ship captain's questionable business association with several powerful peers permitted him the luxury of hovering on *le beau monde's* outer fringes.

The widower would place a few prying questions in the right ears and the truth would out. Then where would she be? She expelled a controlled breath. As long as the captain turned his interest elsewhere, she didn't care what *on dit* the chinwags bandied about. She was made of sterner stuff than that.

Or so she told herself.

A disturbance outside the arbor reined in her musings. The Earl of Luxmoore, the Duke of Harcourt, and Allen crowded into the already overfull bower. A herring-packed tin allowed more room for movement. She wrinkled her nose. And possibly smelled better too.

She sneezed then sneezed again.

"Bless you." Edwina produced a lacy scrap of cloth. "Have you need of a handkerchief?"

"Yes, thank you." Ivonne accepted the linen and pressed it to her nose. The cloth offered some relief from Captain Kirkpatrick's reeking person.

The cozy nook meant for two or three, now teemed with eight bodies, six of whom were muscular males, and one of those rivaled a gorilla in size, smell, and mannerisms.

Ivonne's leg ached, and all of a sudden, she felt somewhat faint. The confined quarters, Falcon's startling announcement, and the captain's belligerent presence, along with her empty stomach, contributed to her light-headedness.

She attempted, without success, to shift away from the mass of bodies.

Captain Kirkpatrick's intimidating form lurked before her.

No reprieve there.

Edmund stood mashed against her on the right.

The arbor's wall hindered movement to her immediate left. Both prevented her from easing away from Falcon's solid form pressing into her from behind.

The latter she didn't mind too much, truth to tell. In fact, the most outlandish urge to lean into him and wiggle her bum plagued her.

How would he react if I did?

The stale air and lack of food must have addled her senses.

Giving herself a mental shake, she peered at the new arrivals. She could scarcely make out who was who within the gloomy interior.

His countenance grim, Allen faced Captain Kirkpatrick. "I've asked you before, as has my father, to direct your attentions elsewhere. My sister is not now, nor will she ever be, available to consider your suit."

The widower's eyes widened before narrowing in suspicion. "Because she's promised to another? Who?"

"I'd say that's a private family matter." Luxmoore flicked something from his shoulder.

A leaf?

A spider?

Were the nasty devils burrowing into her tresses? Ivonne swept her hand across the top of her head, and then through the tangled mass at her nape a couple of times. She'd be hard-pressed to say which she reviled more. ... The captain or the spiders?

"If she's not on the Marriage Mart, why haven't I heard mention of the fact before?" Captain Kirkpatrick crossed his arms and glared round the nook. "Something here is too smoky by far, and I mean to find out what it is."

On second thought, spiders are adorable creatures compared to Kirkpatrick.

"Why don't you do that?" Lord Luxmoore stepped forward. "Elsewhere."

"Yes, a splendid idea." The duke joined Luxmoore beside the widower. "I'm sure there are a multitude of eager gossips within the house willing to assist you with your intrusive meddling."

Each placed a hand on one of the sea captain's arms.

Snarling, he jerked from their holds. He loomed before Ivonne.

Lifting her chin a notch, she forced herself to meet his angry eyes as he towered above her. Marriage to this man was unthinkable. He would terrorize her every day he remained ashore.

"I mean to get to the bottom of this, Miss Wimpleton. I delayed sailing and wasted months courting you with the intention of making you a mother to my sons. I won't be made a fool of."

"Did that by yourself, seems to me," Edmund muttered.

Beside him, Edwina clapped and giggled. "Brilliant, Eddy."

Captain Kirkpatrick rounded on Edmund. "Stubble it, young pup, before I thrash you soundly."

"Do come along, Kirkpatrick." An exaggerated sigh echoed from near the exit, and His Grace beckoned. "I've had quite enough of your Drury Lane theatrics for one evening. ... Unless we need to notify Lord Wimpleton we require a dozen strapping footmen to haul you from the premises."

"You sure a dozen will suffice?" Falcon's jeer resulted in another round of snickers.

"Bloody arses." Spinning on his heel, the captain stomped from the nook.

The duke and earl swung their attention to her brother.

Allen waved them away. "We'll see you inside. Keep an eye on Kirkpatrick, will you?"

With a nod and a half-bow to the ladies, Harcourt and Luxmoore trailed after the grumbling seaman.

"We'll also be going." Edwina's curious gaze swung between Ivonne and Falcon. "I'm sure you've much to discuss."

She didn't move an inch but instead, head angled and finger on her chin, continued to study Ivonne and Falcon. Edwina was too astute by far. "Ivonne, do you—"

"Um, yes," Edmund seized his sister's arm. "We'll let Aunt Mary and Uncle Walter know where you are. Come along, Winnie."

After a cocky salute, he dragged Edwina from the enclosure.

They broke into furious whispers the moment their feet hit the gravel path. What were those two conjuring now?

Ivonne eyed the exit longingly.

This evening had the makings of a Cheltenham Tragedy. She'd been accosted, made an inglorious spectacle of, rescued by the only man who'd ever sent her heart palpitating and nether regions tingling, and she would bet her pin money that within fifteen minutes, her name would buzz about the ballroom thicker than bees on honey.

She wanted nothing more than to sneak in the house's side entrance and flee to her room where she could hide under her bed until next December.

Maybe her parents could be persuaded to depart for Addington Hall early. The social whirl ended in a few weeks in any event. Unless God performed a miracle, she stood no more chance of snaring herself a husband this go round than she had the previous Seasons. She had become an object of scorn and pity.

She would simply refuse to attend another. After all, five stints in Town had quite proved the *bon ton* deemed her an undesirable. Only fortune hunters sought her out, and even they treated her with barely concealed disdain. Allen could contrive some drivel about her phantom intended crying off.

He had eloped with an actress, entered a monastery, had been sat upon by a blind hippopotamus ...

The reason didn't much matter.

Ivonne had long since accepted her fate. Some women were destined to live life alone. Her shoulders slumped. Weariness born more from emotional turmoil than physical fatigue encompassed her.

"If you'll excuse me, I need to repair my appearance." She offered Falcon a brave smile. He would never know how much it cost her to pretend indifference when what she longed to do was throw her arms around his neck, kiss those gorgeous lips of his, and tell him she loved him.

Stop it, goosecap.

He'd made no effort to contact her in six years, and that stung something fierce. No, his indifference had left a deep wound and no small amount of distrust.

"It was wonderful to see you again, Mr. Faulkenhurst."

Should she suggest he call?

No. Likely Allen had already extended an invitation of some sort, which explained Falcon's presence here tonight. Let her brother be the one to issue another. She would only appear desperate to see Falcon again.

Because I am. But to what point?

Waterworks threatened, and Ivonne blinked rapidly. She would not shed another tear for him.

She would not.

"Ivy ...?" He reached for her hand, concern shading his voice.

A single tear trickled a scalding path from the outer corner of her eye. She spun away. Lifting her skirts, she tore from the alcove.

5

Ivy wept.

Chance was certain, although his gut told him her tears couldn't be attributed solely to the captain's boorish behavior.

Allen stared after his sister's fleeing form before facing Chance, a question in his hooded eyes. "I say, what was that about?"

"I'm sure I have no idea why she pelted off in such haste." Raising a brow, Chance met Allen's shuttered scrutiny.

He did, but the niggling thought was scarcely more than a heartbeat. Her response to him hadn't been that of a sister. He needed time to reflect on the notion. He must tread carefully if he had any hope, no matter how remote or seemingly impossible, of making her his.

Staring at the now empty pathway, Chance rubbed the side of his nose. "Perhaps Ivy feared someone would see her in disarray."

"No, not her abrupt departure. I meant telling Kirkpatrick my sister is promised to someone else." Allen eyed him, expectancy written on his features.

Damn, Allen wouldn't let that falsehood go unaccounted for.

"Ah, that." Chance offered a weak chuckle. "Not one of my cleverer moments, I'll confess."

He traced the scar on his cheek, recalling Ivy's gentle touch. She hadn't seemed the least repulsed by the jagged mark.

"I said the one thing I thought would make the boor leave off pursuing her." He didn't elaborate how he'd bitten his tongue to keep from saying, "Promised to *me*."

If only he'd dared to. What would have happened?

Mrs. Washburn's freckled face, immediately followed by his sire's disproving countenance, flashed to mind. Hell, with that ridiculous millstone about his neck, Chance must proceed with the greatest of caution.

He rubbed his arm then his hand. He might indulge in a bit of laudanum tonight—to take the edge off the pain. More on point, the drug would numb his mind and the tormenting thoughts of Ivy, which guaranteed another sleepless night.

Allen drew in a gusty breath and ran his hand through his dark hair. "I'm heartily sick of the captain, I can tell you. I don't trust the sod one whit. He'll not let this fabricated affiancing story die a quiet death. Of that I'm positive."

"Why is he here tonight if you and Ivy find him so offensive?" Chance's arm throbbed. He needed to say his farewells soon. "Did your mother invite him?"

Allen snorted. "Absolutely not. Mother cannot abide Kirkpatrick, either. The bugger hangs on the coat sleeves of others. I'm sure he wrangled an invitation to accompany one of his business cronies."

Allen exited the bower ahead of Chance.

"I'll speak to Mother. I'm thinking she needs to

further refine her guest list."

"Indeed." Chance followed him outside, grateful for the fresh air filling his lungs. He'd guess no part of Kirkpatrick had seen the inside of a tub in a good while. Imagining Ivy with the man set Chance's teeth on edge once again.

"So, this is where you got off to." Grinning, Allen gestured toward the alcove. "Thought you were in the library, but when I checked, you'd disappeared. I wondered where you'd sequestered yourself."

He threw an arm across Chance's shoulders. "No need to hide, Faulkenhurst."

Chance winced as pain speared his arm and hand. "I wasn't hiding. I wanted to reacquaint myself with the grounds, and you have to admit, the air within the house is intolerable."

Not nearly as intolerable as the arbor.

Truth to tell, he had been avoiding the throng inside the manor.

He'd arrived this evening, terrified he'd encounter Ivy and equally desperate to do so. He hadn't expected her to dash into the bower while he lurked there. Rather awkward to be caught skulking in the garden alcove. He'd opened his mouth to tell her he stood behind her when the sea crab appeared.

Her fear of the man tangible, Ivy had needed safeguarding. So, Chance remained silent and, in some measure, grateful he had a legitimate reason not to return to the ball.

Pasting a fake smile on his face and pretending nonchalance about his crippling injuries took a greater toll than he'd imagined they would. He'd endured more pitying glances and ignored more horrified gasps and looks of revulsion than anyone ought to in a single night.

Wonder what long-toothed Mrs. Washburn and her father will think of my condition?

Didn't matter what they thought. Chance had no intention of honoring his father's ludicrous proposal. Although the blame for the bumblebroth lay at Father's feet, the delicate situation needed discrete handling.

Excusing himself from the ball early on, Chance had drifted to the library. Reading had proved futile. Laying the book aside, he'd wandered to the French windows and stared blankly at the night. The lure of the arbor called him.

He'd been unable to resist a visit to another time, when he'd dreamed Ivy might be his. She'd dwelled in his thoughts, and though he'd been no monk, he'd never desired another as much as her.

When a man gave his heart to a woman, other females might temporarily satiate his physical desire, but his soul continued to yearn for its mate, seeking the wholeness no other could offer.

Yesterday, when Allen insisted he join him at his table at White's, Chance had posed several subtle questions regarding the family's health, business ventures, and finally, he'd dared to inquire about Ivy.

Allen had smiled knowingly, as if he'd expected the conversation to shift to a discussion about his sister. Peculiar that. Chance had never confided in his long-time friend, never hinted he held Ivy in any special regard. He couldn't contain his broad smile or the joy that had swept him upon learning she remained unmarried.

"There's no shortage of damsels inside eager for

dance partners." His arm about Chance's shoulders, Allen set their course toward the bustling mansion. "Unless you forgot how to perform *Mr. Beveridge's Maggot* in the wilds of India."

Chance didn't want to dance with those ladies. A sable-haired, hazel-eyed sprite with a beauty mark beside her left nostril was the only woman he ever wanted to hold in his arms. And if he'd heard correctly in the arbor, she didn't dance anymore.

"I'll tell you, I could use a stiff swallow of French brandy after that nonsense with Kirkpatrick." Allen withdrew his arm and quickened his pace.

Their shoes clicked on the limestone pavers as they neared the house.

"I'd not say no to a nip of cognac," Chance admitted.

"Let's find you a dance partner, and I'll make sure the Jack Nasty Face took his leave." Allen tossed Chance a familiar teasing grin. "Then we'll both indulge in a finger's worth or two."

The drink sounded wonderful.

The dance Chance would pass on. Dancing required the touching of hands.

Allen's grin widened. "I do believe that scar on your cheek improves your devilish good looks. Makes you seem mysterious and debonair. Second son or not, the ladies will be vying for your attention."

Chance stopped and yanked off his modified glove. He raised his disfigured hand. "Even with this? I think you over-estimate my attraction, my friend."

"Does it pain you still?" Brow creased, Allen stared at the two nubs where Chance's middle and forefinger used to be.

A long, jagged scar disappeared into the wristband of his coat sleeve.

"Some. It's been less than six months." He tugged the glove on, not without some difficulty. Thank God Allen didn't offer to help. Chance crooked his lips upward.

"You should see the scar on my forearm. Nearly lost the thing. I imagine I look a bit like that creature in that new novel. What's it called?"

He sent a contemplative glance skyward.

"Ah, I remember." Chance lowered his voice to an

eerie growl. "*Frankenstein.*"

Allen's expression grew serious. "Don't be absurd. Mangled arm and minus two fingers, you're more of a man than ninety percent of the coves here tonight."

"Only ninety?" Chance quipped to hide the emotion Allen's kind words aroused.

Lost in thought, Chance ascended the terrace steps. The veranda swarmed with guests, no doubt seeking fresh air.

Allen stopped on the top riser and gave him a broad grin. "I've missed you, Falcon. We all have."

"There you are, Allen, Faulkenhurst." Lord Wimpleton, his usually jovial countenance severe, strode in their direction. Upon reaching them, he gave a cursory glance around.

No one paid them any mind.

His brow furrowed, the viscount dropped his voice. "Please explain to me if either of you have the slightest idea why, in the last ten minutes, I've had several guests offer me congratulations on my daughter's betrothal."

6

Edging the library's terrace door open a crack, Ivonne peered inside.

No one.

A single lamp burned low atop the mantle. A leather volume lay open on the dark puce and ebony settee. Odd. Who would have been in here tonight? One didn't attend a ball with the intention of seeking a spot to read.

Someone chose to avoid the gathering. Why?

She slipped inside, closing the door behind her. The latch sank home with a soft click. She still clutched Edwina's wadded handkerchief. Ivonne smiled wryly and tucked the cloth inside her bodice. Rushing to the other entrance, her emerald satin slippers scuffed atop the Axminster carpet.

Her gaze fell on her reflection in the oval mirror positioned above a mahogany drum table, and she faltered to a sudden stop. Gads, her appearance bordered on indecent. Without much stretch of the imagination, guests might ponder if she'd indulged in a dalliance in the garden.

Ivonne raised a hand to the hair trailing down her spine and over her left shoulder and plucked two small leaves from the tendrils. Glancing down, she sighed. A torn piece of black netting dangled above her hemline. Bending, she inspected the tear.

Not awful. A few artful stitches ought to repair the rip.

Should she seek her chamber on the third floor or the lady's retiring room just down the hall? The retiring room seemed the more logical choice to set herself aright. Except ... what if other ladies occupied the chamber? How would she explain her unkempt appearance? The gossip coffers already overflowed on her behalf tonight.

She shrugged. So be it.

She would tell any ladies in the room that she took a spill into the shrubberies. Given her penchant for tripping and stumbling, no one ought to question the taradiddle.

Ivonne cracked open the door and took a furtive peek up and down the hall.

All clear.

She hurried the few yards to the retiring room. Taking a deep breath, she pasted a smile on her face and pressed the lever down. The door swung open.

Empty, thank goodness. Not even a maid.

Where was Barrett? It wasn't like the servant to leave her post.

Grateful for the reprieve Ivonne stepped inside and closed her eyes for a long moment. She took a steadying breath—the first relaxed one she'd enjoyed since tearing from the terrace.

Chancey Faulkenhurst.

Falcon.

His handsome face forced its way to the forefront of her mind. After all this time, he'd returned. Her imprudent heart beat faster. Why did he have to return now, when she'd finally put him behind her? When she was crippled and considered past her prime? When he could never be hers?

Ivonne opened her eyes and shook her head. A rose petal floated to the floor. His homecoming changed nothing.

Locating a table with mirrors, assorted fripperies, hair pins, and such, she took a seat. After yanking off her gloves, she set them aside and went about haphazardly repinning her mass of hair.

Falcon had spent many hours in the garden nook with her—until he'd left for India. She had pleaded with her parents for two weeks straight before they finally relented and gave her permission to correspond with him, as long as they read every letter first.

A flush of chagrin heated her face. What they must have thought. She'd been such a fawning, green girl.

She'd not heard from Falcon once during his absence. Not a single page, though she'd written to him every week the first year. At sixteen, she'd believed her heart would never recover when she finally accepted he wasn't going to answer her letters. She'd brooded about in a fit of the blue devils for months.

If he'd cared an iota for her, he would have written. Not a single line in six years sent an indisputable message. He wasn't interested. She was no featherbrain. She'd misinterpreted his kindness and thoughtfulness for something more.

Something which would never be.

Ivonne had come to realize her childish dream of marrying him had been just that: a silly, unattainable fantasy. Somehow, the knowledge alleviated her girlish infatuation, although over the years, she hadn't become enamored of anyone else. Nor had she encouraged other suitors' attentions either—not that there'd been a horde of them to begin with.

Nonetheless, a part of her heart would always belong to Falcon. She had resolutely tucked that piece away and refused to extract the fragment from its snug resting place. The remainder of her heart she kept guarded, not willing to suffer such torment again. Once in a lifetime was quite enough, thank you.

As much as she once adored him, years' worth of callous indifference had created a chasm between them. She would never trust her emotions again, especially not love.

She supposed that's why she'd been accused of being unapproachable and standoffish.

On one occasion, she overheard a group of gentlemen suggest that the swan ice sculpture their hosts commissioned for the Yuletide gala possessed more personality and warmth than she. One dandy had mockingly called her Icy Ivonne. The others sniggered in obvious agreement.

Truth to tell, she compared every man to Falcon, and all came up wanting.

She paused and stared at her reflection in the mirror.

The woman peering back at her wasn't disagreeable nor was she particularly noteworthy. Clear hazel eyes, more oval than round and almost green in the candlelight, were her best feature besides her alabaster skin. A rather square chin, pert mouth with too full lips, and straight dark hair of a nondescript shade of brown completed her inventory.

No, a diamond of the first water she wasn't. Falcon possessed the beauty she lacked. Men weren't supposed to be beautiful, but to describe him otherwise, didn't do him justice.

No other male possessed eyes quite the same gray-blue as he, like the sea after a mighty winter tempest. A hint of humor and kindness always glimmered in their thick-lashed depths. High cheekbones and a straight aristocratic nose, combined with those sculpted lips and his dark blond hair streaked with gold ... she released a long, shuddering breath.

He was as close to Adonis in the flesh as she'd ever seen. She'd been paraded before young dandies and bucks aplenty, and although handsome, some profoundly so, all paled in comparison to Falcon.

Ivonne frowned.

He bore a fresh scar on his cheek. In the arbor's muted light, the mark barely showed. His hair had gleamed gold, more than she remembered, though his eyes seemed darker.

Cooler. Distant.

Icy Ivonne she might be, but Falcon's smile possessed the ability to transform her into a mass of melted flummery. Only, now, she neared her third and twentieth birthday and no longer wore her emotions on her sleeve like a flighty girl.

He'd never learn how he affected her.

Securing the last pin, she scrutinized her attempt to repair her coiffure. She patted the back of her head, unable to tell if all her hair was in place. True, the style wasn't the elaborate coiled knot Dawson created earlier this evening, but at least her locks weren't tumbling down her back in shocking disarray.

Ivonne twisted to examine the chamber. Where were the sewing supplies?

The door flew open and several women filed in.

Lydia Farnsworth smiled kindly before disappearing behind a screen.

The Dundercroft sisters, Francine and Lyselle, tripped to a stop, as did their constant companion, Penelope Rossington.

Perfect.

Three of London's worst rumormongers with scarcely a speck of common sense amongst them.

Barrett scooted past the ladies. She dipped a curtsy.

"Oh, Miss Wimpleton, please excuse my absence. I had to fetch more towels." She lifted the stack of snowy cloths she held. "The ladies have suffered dreadfully from the heat this evening."

Ivonne smiled. "It's quite all right. I need to mend my gown. It sustained a minor tear when I was in the garden."

A petite, shapely blonde, Miss Rossington glided further into the room. Uncommonly attractive, she knew it well.

Ivonne stifled a gasp. Had Miss Rossington dampened her gown?

That's what came of having no mother, an overindulgent father, and the morals of a barnyard cat.

Ivonne's modest endowments appeared childlike next to such curvaceousness. Of course, if she puffed her chest out in the same manner, she'd appear more buxom too. Walking about aiming one's bosoms skyward must cause a fierce backache and wreak havoc on one's balance.

Not worth the discomfort or danger.

She prayed the attention Allen directed toward Miss Rossington was driven by politeness and not any intent on his part to court the wench. A slight shudder shook her. A worse sister-in-law she couldn't imagine.

"Whatever were you doing that you tore your gown, Miss Wimpleton?" Miss Rossington's gaze focused on the mirror behind Ivonne. Her citrine eyes—the exact same shade as Ivonne's ancient cat, Sir Pounce—rounded. A smirk curved Miss Rossington's ruby-tinted lips.

Captain Kirkpatrick. Blast him to Hades.

The freckled Dundercroft misses tittered behind their pudgy hands.

Ivonne stared at the trio, a chill causing the flesh on her arms to pucker.

What Banbury Tales had the captain concocted when he'd come inside? Alarm and shame engulfed her. What would she say to her parents? How could she explain this bumblebroth away without partially blaming Falcon for claiming she was promised?

"Is it true?" Miss Rossington advanced another few mincing steps. She cast her cohorts a secretive smile. "You've managed to get yourself affianced at *long* last?"

Heaven help me.

"I ..." Ivonne swallowed, dread drying her mouth. She loathed lying.

"Who is he?" Envy twisted the corners of the elder Miss Dundercroft's thin lips.

"Yes, do tell." Miss Lyselle fairly danced in anticipation. Her plump bosoms and curls bounced with her excitement. She clapped her hands together. "Do we know him? Is he here tonight?"

"Is that why you've shrubbery in your mussed hair and your dress is torn?" Miss Rossington swept her hand across her perfectly styled flaxen hair. Her diamond and sapphire bracelet shimmered in the candlelight. She smiled, a malicious glint in her feline eyes.

She tittered unkindly. "Your hair looks like an owl in an ivy bush ... *a-la-blowze.*"

Poufy? Still?

Ivonne touched her hair and peered into the mirror over her shoulder.

Miss Rossington snuck up behind her. In one deft

move, she plucked something from Ivonne's hair. She displayed the coral petal for the others to see.

A fresh round of giggles erupted from the Dundercrofts. Glee pinkened their already ruddy complexions. Bright red blotches covered their faces, chests, and arms.

Miss Kingsley appeared behind them.

Ivonne's breath caught. She was in attendance tonight? Did Allen know? When had she arrived?

An exquisite redhead, the woman had been in the Caribbean with her brother and father for the past three years. At one time, Ivonne had thought Allen enamored of the beauty.

"Really, *girls*." Miss Kingsley emphasized the word, indicating what she thought of them and staring pointedly at Miss Rossington. "I'm certain if Lord and Lady Wimpleton wanted their guests to know Miss Wimpleton's joyous news, they'd make an announcement this evening."

No condemnation in her gaze, she flashed Ivonne a brilliant smile. "Sometimes, people prefer to keep the arrangements to themselves for a time. A promise to marry is, after all, a very special occurrence, and one to cherish, not toss about like a shuttlecock during a game."

Miss Rossington's face flamed, and she scowled at Miss Kingsley.

"Don't you agree, Miss Rossington?" Miss Kingsley tilted her head, a secretive smile curving her lips.

Miss Rossington suddenly became fixated with her bracelet.

Ivonne couldn't recall a time when the chit didn't have some sort of sharp retort on the tip of her tongue.

Lydia Farnsworth emerged from behind the screen. "Miss Wimpleton, if you'll permit me, you've a few leaves and rose petals in your hair."

She pointed to Ivonne's head. "Just there, below your crown."

Ivonne braved a smile. No doubt they considered her a promiscuous tart now that she was supposedly betrothed. She couldn't refute a word of it. She nodded and turned to face the mirror once more. "If you would be so kind."

After giving Ivonne a reassuring smile and skimming her gaze over Miss Rossington, who glared daggers, Miss Kingsley took her turn behind the painted screen.

Through lowered lashes, Ivonne observed Miss Rossington in the mirror's reflection. She sank gracefully into a chair before another mirror at the same table where Ivonne sat. The Dundercrofts huddled on either side like dumpy sentinels.

Two other tables and she must choose to sit at this one?

A smug smile stretched Miss Rossington's lips, exposing her perfect teeth.

What, no feline incisors? No claws hidden inside her gloves or tail twitching beneath her skirt? No hissing or scratching? No gagging and choking on an enormous, hairball, more's the pity?

"Mr. Faulkenhurst is in attendance this evening," Miss Rossington fairly purred as she removed her gloves and sent a sideways glance toward the screen.

Ah, baring our claws now, are we?

Her cat eyes narrowed. "Newly arrived from India, I believe."

"Oh, he's a handsome one." Miss Lyselle sighed, a dreamy expression on her chubby face.

"No, dear, he won't do at all." Miss Dundercroft admonished her younger sister with a stern stare. "Not only is he a penniless second son," disgust pinched her mouth, "the man's disfigured."

How dare she?

Ivonne straightened her spine, prepared to give the haughty chit a proper set down. "He most certain—"

"They say," Miss Rossington ran her fingers along her fan's carved ivory guard, her sultry gaze affixed on Ivonne, "he lost his *manhood* to those barbarians."

7

The Wimpletons' mahogany longcase clock chimed the early morning hour of two. Legs stretched before him and his ankles crossed, Chance settled further into the leather wingback chair before the library's blazing hearth. He took a long pull from the glass he held, welcoming the brandy's heat sluicing to his gut.

In the silence of the slumbering household, he'd grown chilled.

The house proved drafty, and London's temperatures were far cooler than those he'd become accustomed to in India. He'd forgotten how penetrating the damp could be. After asking a footman to light the logs arranged in the Rumford fireplace, Chance had spent the last hour staring into the soothing, hypnotic flames.

Yesterday, he'd gratefully accepted Allen's invitation to stay with the Wimpletons until he became settled in England. Chance boasted no residence of his own in London, and although he could open his brother's house in Mayfair, that seemed more bother than necessary. Especially since Chance didn't know how long he'd be in Town. He had several business dealings to attend to before he trotted off to Suttoncliffe Hall and surprised his family.

He hadn't written to inform them of his return or that he'd been injured. They had worries enough of their own. Thad, his brother, and Thad's wife expected their first child any day, and Chance's sister, Annabel, had her hands full with her scapegrace of a husband.

The rhythmic *tick-tocking* of the clock beckoned sleep, yet slumber eluded Chance as it often had these past months. When he drifted into a fitful rest, nightmares awakened him. Drenched in sweat, his heart pounding with the force of a blacksmith's hammer against an anvil, he'd stare into the darkness until the horrific visions faded into the shadows of his mind.

Concentrating on Ivy's serene features, sweet smile, and the dimple in her right cheek banished the memories until sleep seduced him once more.

A greater concern this night was the damage Kirkpatrick's jealousy and flapping tongue had caused. Not only had he stretched Chance's suggestion that Ivy was promised to another into a full-fledged contracted betrothal, the blackguard had suggested the wedding would take place within a month or two.

As Chance came in from the terrace, he overheard the captain speaking to a small crowd

"Lord Wimpleton insists the announcement will be forthcoming any day," Kirkpatrick said.

Lying cawker.

At Chance's behest, Sethwick questioned the captain. "How is it you are privy to such intimate information?"

Kirkpatrick told Sethwick, in addition to several other guests, "Lord Wimpleton requested an audience with me the moment I reentered the ballroom."

What drivel.

According to Captain Kirkpatrick, Lord Wimpleton apologized for his daughter's fast behavior as well as leading the poor widower on.

"My daughter knows full well I negotiated a settlement with another gentleman long before either she or I made your acquaintance, Captain Kirkpatrick. Please accept my humblest apologies, and rest assured, if she were not already spoken for, I would be most happy to consider your offer."

Blatant lies, according to Allen and his father.

Recalling the conversation, Chance scowled.

If Kirkpatrick couldn't have Ivy, he was determined no one else should either. He'd backed Lord Wimpleton and her into a corner. Either they produce her intended or henceforth be labeled liars.

And the fault was Chance's.

Intent on protecting her, he'd lost control for one brief moment.

God Almighty, he'd only made matters worse, bloody fool. Guilt and remorse gnawed at him. He examined every angle of the situation, trying to arrive at an amenable solution. If only he were unencumbered ... *and wealthy*.

THE LIEUTENANT AND THE LADY

He shut his eyes against the remorse. Ivy's features immediately floated before him.

She had blossomed into a rare beauty. He'd known she would.

Her hair, the richest sable, had been as silky beneath his chin as he'd imagined. Her pearly skin, smoother than a rose petal, begged to be touched. Her thick-lashed eyes, stormy-sky gray one minute and sage green with silvery flecks the next, reflected the peace of the deepest forest. And her lips, full and luscious, would have tempted Adam in the Garden of Eden.

Not the typical *haut ton* measure of loveliness, no, his Ivy was something far more exceptional. An unpretentious dove amongst strutting peacocks and brazen parrots.

Opening his eyes, Chance twisted his mouth into a smirk. Drink had him waxing poetic.

He swirled the glass of cognac. The fire's glow lightened the brandy's umber hue to mellow amber. He'd indulged more than he ought, but he'd changed his mind about taking a dose of laudanum.

While abroad, he'd seen too many opium addicts and detested using the tincture. A dram or two of strong spirits proved a better choice to induce sleep. His lips curled into a self-deprecatory smile. The three prior glasses of brandy he'd imbibed could hardly be considered medicinal.

He uncrossed his ankles and laid his head against the chair's high back, watching the fire's shadows dance and stretch across the ceiling.

The boring-as-stale-bread novel he'd attempted to read earlier lay unopened on the table beside him. Chance drummed his fingers on the chair's arm. He ached to play the piano in the drawing room. A consummate pianist in his youth, these past six years there'd been few opportunities to indulge in the pleasurable pastime.

Despite his father's adamant disapproval of Chance's *womanish obsession*, his mother had encouraged his playing. Then Mother died, and Father began pressuring him to find a suitable wife.

One with a nice, fat purse.

He didn't want to wed any woman except Ivy.

Right before he'd left for India, he'd approached Lord Wimpleton and asked for her hand.

The man had laughed, though not unkindly. "My daughter's much too young for me to consider any talk of marriage. Return when she's older and you have something besides a besotted heart to offer her. Then, I'll consider your suit."

Offer her? What?

A fortune.

How?

India.

More than a few nabobs had purchased a seat in Parliament and risen to the *ton's* top tiers after acquiring a fortune via trade with India. Chance possessed no interest in Parliament or government, but he had hoped to become modestly prosperous. Enough that Lord Wimpleton would consider granting him his daughter's hand in marriage.

Unfortunately, his duties for the East India Company Troops allowed minimal time for business ventures. Aside from a single investment he'd made with a British businessman, Clement Robinson, when Chance first arrived in Madras, no further opportunities to pursue that avenue had arisen.

Not long after meeting Robinson, Chance had been transferred to Calcutta and then moved to four other provinces, each remoter than the last. He'd eventually arrived in Maratha Territory, where he'd been gravely wounded.

Although he'd attempted to reach Robinson several times, after two years without success, Chance gave up. He'd been made a May Game of, and the paltry inheritance Mother left him had been stolen by an unscrupulous scoundrel.

So, Chance had stayed in India. His aspirations of marrying Ivy shriveled into crumbs of crushed hope, and the arid desert winds scattered them into oblivion. If he couldn't make her his wife, he wouldn't wed at all.

An unpleasant notion burst into his thoughts.

Bloody hell.

What if Lambert or Mrs. Washburn had yammered about the proposed union between Chance and her? He would have written and told his father he refused the match, except the postal service in the remote provinces wasn't to be relied upon.

Due to the frequent movement of East India Troops, mail delivery was delayed or, oftentimes, didn't reach the person intended at all. In fact, Chance hadn't received the first of Ivy's correspondences until after he'd lost what meager monies he had possessed. He had nothing to offer her and did what he believed best: ignored her letters, telling himself she would soon find someone to give her heart to.

Except she hasn't give her heart to anyone in all this time. Why?

Splaying the fingers of his ruined hand, he stared at the empty space where the digits ought to be. Peculiarly, but he felt them at times. They itched, ached, twitched—not in actuality, of course, but phantom sensations of what once was. At times, he even tried to pick up items with the missing appendages.

Losing himself in the magic of music had been his singular passion, other than Ivy. Now, both were lost to him.

Sighing, he set aside the brandy. Brooding served

no purpose. After shoving to his feet, he banked the fire before circling the room and blowing out the candles, except one three-branched candelabrum. A final glance at the fireplace assured him the meshed brass guard prevented embers from escaping.

Determined to put the day behind him, he snatched the candelabrum and exited the room. Across the hall, the drawing room door stood open. Lid closed, the grand piano washed in the moon's silvery glow beckoned him. He stood in the doorway for several long minutes, his emotions vacillating.

A scan of the corridor confirmed Chance alone remained below at this ungodly hour. He advanced into the room, standing unsure for a moment. He placed the candles atop the piano and ran a hand along the carved mahogany. A truly grand instrument.

After shrugging out of his coat, he tossed the cutaway on a needlepoint parlor chair. Before he sat, he unbuttoned his shirtsleeves and rolled them to his elbows. The ivory keys gleamed in the soft light. He rested a tentative hand upon their surface, relishing their familiar cool presence beneath his fingertips.

His useless left hand lay on his thigh. He ran his right fingertips across the keys and, pressing the quiet pedal with his foot, played a familiar melody, one-handed.

"Falcon?" Ivy whispered his name, her voice a blend of curiosity and wonder.

8

Ivonne tossed the bedcovers off and sat up.
What was the time?

After lighting a candle, she examined the bedside clock. Past two.

Releasing a beleaguered sigh, she flopped onto her back. She would be a sleep-deprived disaster in the morning. Maybe she would stay in bed the entire day and wallow in her doldrums.

Miss Rossington's shocking revelation about Falcon had made sleep impossible. Ivonne hadn't been capable of returning to the ball either. She feared the moment she laid eyes on him, she would burst into tears. Learning of his shattering injury from Miss Rossington—of all people—was beyond the pale. Feigning a headache, Ivonne had bolted to her bedchamber.

She eyed the clock again.

A trip below stairs was in order. Father possessed a number of yawn-inspiring books. She would select the most boring tome on philosophy the library had to offer—Descartes or Hume would do nicely—and be asleep within fifteen minutes.

Common sense halted her halfway out the bedchamber door. She wore nothing but her lacy nightgown. Gads. That wouldn't do. Snatching her robe from the foot of the bed, she paused. What if someone else prowled about below? Not likely at this hour.

It mattered not. She required a tedious book to put her to sleep.

Ivonne shoved her arms into the sleeves. Silver candleholder in hand, she made for the library. Halting piano music lured her into the drawing room.

Falcon sat before the instrument, utter defeat in his hunched shoulders and dejected profile.

Lonely, lost soul.

Her heart wrenched.

"Falcon?"

He stopped playing the instant she uttered his name. Turning his head, he faced her. Vulnerability tinged with embarrassment lingered in his gaze. His beautiful eyes searched hers.

What did he seek?

Pity? Compassion? Sympathy?

Each overwhelmed her, but he didn't need those emotions at present.

He required hope. Acceptance. Strength. *Love.*

Falcon's keen focus sank to her attire then to her bare toes. His lips twitched, and warmth swept her cheeks.

At least she'd thought to throw on her robe. Appearing before a gentleman in her nightwear with her unruly hair billowing about her shoulders was most improper. Truth to tell, at the moment, she didn't care. The lavender silk nightgown and robe swished around her ankles and calves as she hurried to him. Her cold feet sank into the lush carpet.

Ivonne placed her candlestick next to the other candleholder atop the piano. Ignoring wisdom, she sank onto the bench beside him. The heat of his solid thigh wedged against hers sent a strange shock along her nerves.

Neither of them made an effort to put a suitable distance between them. But then, nothing about being here in the middle of the night clothed in a diaphanous nightgown and robe, unchaperoned to boot, could be considered remotely acceptable.

If caught, she would be ruined.

She gave a mental shrug. That didn't matter. Everything in her ached to be with Falcon, to seize whatever precious moments destiny afforded her. Ivonne's need to be with him at this moment shoved aside the sting of his prior disinterest.

Drinking in his features, her focus hovered on the fresh scar marring his handsome face. She longed to kiss the pinkish mark, to somehow convey that she found knowing he'd suffered excruciating to bear.

God above, she'd missed him.

Her eyes misting with tears, she directed her attention to his hands lest she cause him more discomfit. She gasped, barely suppressing the cry surging to her throat.

His poor hand.

Falcon made no attempt to hide it.

Ivonne blinked away burning tears.

Two fingers. Gone. Falcon, a gifted pianist, would make music no more.

Lifting her gaze to his, she forced a facade of composure.

He returned her regard, his gaze guarded and appraising. This was not the carefree, jovial individual she'd known most of her life. He'd suffered, and suffered greatly. What happened in India to change him thus?

"How ...?" She cleared her throat, determined to show the same fortitude he did. She deliberately didn't return her scrutiny to his hand. No doubt, he was self-conscious enough already. "How did you come by your injury?"

Lifting the limb, he allowed her to see the vicious scar disfiguring his arm from hand to elbow.

She reached to touch the puckered flesh, but hesitated. He didn't pull away. Ever-so-gently, she trailed her fingers along the rough skin.

Dear God, the agony he must have endured.

Fresh tears sprang to her eyes. She swallowed them away. "Does it hurt terribly?"

Falcon shrugged, his broad shoulders bunching beneath the light linen shirt.

"Sometimes more than others." He flexed his remaining fingers. "My movement improves daily."

He lost his manhood.

Miss Rossington's acrimonious words echoed in Ivonne's mind.

"Do you have ... other wounds?" She practically ground her teeth in vexation.

Curse her wagging tongue. Of course he does, dimwit. Do you expect him to blurt the God-awful truth about his ... his ... maleness?

He turned his arm over so she could see the other side. The wound wrapped around his forearm, a reddish-purple serpent of mutilated flesh. "I've a few others, mostly on my ribs and back."

"What happened?" Ivonne didn't want him to tell her what trauma he'd undergone. Her heart could barely tolerate seeing these scars. Somehow, she sensed he needed to talk of the experience in order to put the ordeal behind him. To heal in his soul as well as his body.

"My commander ordered us to surround and invade the Pindaris." Falcon sighed and gave her a sideways look. His handsome mouth twisted into a wry grimace. "I tried to save a woman and her four children trapped inside their burning home. Two Pindari attacked me before I could get the last boy out."

His eyes darkened to midnight, and grief hardened his features. "The Pindaris' homes were destroyed. Burned to the ground, every one."

The muscles in his jaw taut, he closed his eyes for a lengthy moment.

"Not a day passes that I don't regret requesting a transfer to India. The devastation some British have inflicted on those unfortunate people, caused by insatiable greed for land and resources ..."

"It sounds absolutely horrid." Ivonne laid her hand on his arm, the flesh warm and rough beneath her palm. "You couldn't have known what to expect."

Why had he asked to go to India in the first place?

He'd never told her. Never said how long he'd be gone. Or if he planned on returning. Ever. Every day, she'd prayed for his safety, forcing away her feelings of betrayal and despondency.

A thought struck Ivonne, the absolute certainty of the epiphany penetrating to her soul. The knowledge left her flabbergasted, and the air hitched in her lungs, all the more proof she had hit upon the truth. She caressed his beautiful face with her gaze.

She'd waited for him, secretly hopeful he'd return someday. And that maybe, by some miracle of providence or God's grace, he'd missed her as much as she'd missed him. That was why she hadn't entertained the attentions of other beaus.

She'd been waiting for Falcon's homecoming.

His eyes hooded, a slow, sensual smile curved his mouth.

Did he know? Had he guessed? How could he have?

She dropped her attention to the piano, afraid he'd read the truth in her eyes.

Men as handsome as he didn't settle for spinsterish misses like her. No, they drew diamonds of the first water to them as naturally and uncontrollably as the moon's irresistible draw upon the tide. Beauty sought beauty. Each to their own kind.

The injustice of that reality didn't escape her.

"May I ask you something?" Falcon brushed a lock of hair off her cheek.

Oh, to have the right to turn her face into his hand and press her lips to his palm.

"Of course." In the faint candlelight, he was even more striking than she'd remembered. "What is it you wish to know?

"In the arbor, Kirkpatrick spoke of your limp. What happened?"

Ivonne gathered her hair and twisted the mass into a thick rope before draping it across her shoulder.

"I broke my leg in two places, the result of a riding accident." She toyed with the ends of her hair. "One break didn't heal properly."

Falcon inclined his head in the direction she'd come from moments before. "I didn't notice a limp just now."

"It's less noticeable on soft surfaces and if my leg is rested."

Enough talk about her. She wanted to learn what his plans were. More specifically, where would he make his home? Would he take a wife?

The notion, as unsavory as tainted fish, coiled in her stomach.

She absently played a couple of chords with her left hand and then began fingering the bass line of a favorite sonata. "What will you do now?"

9

"**D**o you have any plans?"

Ivonne asked the question burning on her lips since she'd bumped into Falcon in the garden. Why hadn't he traveled straight to his family estate, Suttoncliffe Hall, instead of choosing to stay in London? After all, he hadn't seen his family in over half a decade.

He tapped out the right hand accompaniment to her chord progression.

A nascent smile bent her mouth. They played rather well together.

His playing became stronger as he slid her a sideways glance. "I'm not altogether certain what I'll do. It depends on several things."

Falcon stopped playing. His stare intense, he stroked her cheek with the back of his good hand, and his attention sank to her mouth.

She sighed and closed her eyes, angling her face into his palm. His touch never failed to send her senses reeling.

"Such as?" My, she was brazen tonight.

"You."

Ivonne's eyes fluttered open. She played a part in what he intended to do?

Dear God, please let him feel something more than friendship toward me.

"Me?" Was that husky voice hers? She couldn't tear her gaze from his parted mouth.

He traced her lips with his rough thumb.

"Why me?" she managed to whisper, fighting the urge to touch his thumb with her tongue.

He didn't answer. Instead, he lowered his head, bit by bit, as she angled her chin upward. Cupping her nape with one hand, he wrapped the other in her long tresses, trapping her.

He was so close. She smelled brandy on his breath

and the faint remains of his woodsy cologne. Every nerve tingled in anticipation.

"Ivy?"

She trembled at the husky timbre of Falcon's voice. Heat suffused her, a delicious, heady warmth spreading from her middle outward, hardening her nipples and causing a curious ache between her legs.

"Yes?" She clutched his solid biceps to keep from melting onto the floor. Did the man have a soft spot anywhere?

"I want to kiss you."

Not more than an inch separated their lips.

"Yes." She dared not breathe, having waited for this moment for so long. Nothing must disturb the magic.

"You're sure?" His nostrils flared, and his hot gaze fastened on her lips. Ever the gentleman, Falcon paused and lifted heavy-lidded eyes to hers. He brushed her lower lip with his thumb again. "You want me to continue?"

Woman's intuition told her he asked for much more than a kiss or two. Ivonne smiled, past caring if he discovered the secret she'd long nurtured in her soul. "I've waited a lifetime to kiss you."

The smile he gave her set her pulse careening. His lips met hers, firm yet gentle at the same time. He shifted his arms, encircling her and lifting her closer.

She entwined her arms around his neck, snuggling against his chest, her aching breasts mashed flat.

He kissed each corner of her mouth then nudged her lips apart with his tongue.

A contented sigh escaped her.

No other suitors' fumbling attempts to kiss her had prepared her for Falcon's seductive assault on her untried senses. Light-headed, swept away on unfamiliar sensation, she parted her lips, granting him access. She was his to do with as he pleased.

He cupped one breast, gently twisting the nipple between his thumb and forefinger as he swept her mouth with his tongue.

She groaned, arching into his hand and meeting his thrusting tongue with her own. Coherent thought flew in the face of her passion. This was all that mattered. Being here with Falcon, finally experiencing what she'd dreamed of for years.

He bent his neck, feathering her throat with scorching kisses before nudging aside the satin of her gown and settling his lips around a swollen nipple.

Head thrown back, Ivonne clung to him, savoring the experience and storing away precious memories. The tender exploration of her breast with his mouth and tongue undid her. When he abandoned her breast, she almost cried out in protest. Then he nuzzled her neck, trailing delicate kisses across her jaw and cheek.

This wonderful, tender man would never be a father.

Joy mingled with sharp sorrow ravaged her emotions. Scalding tears slid from her eyes.

"You're crying?" Falcon stiffened and leaned away, examining her. A shuttered expression settled on his face. "I apologize. I oughtn't to have kissed you."

He shifted, preparing to stand.

"No, Falcon. I wanted you to."

With a volition of its own, her gaze skimmed his wounds. "It's just that you ..."

She couldn't explain her heartache to him. For

him. That she grieved because he'd returned from India a partial man. To do so would cause him more pain and humiliation.

He stood, his face an impassive mask.

"I believe I understand perfectly, Miss Wimpleton. Once I satisfied your schoolgirl curiosity about kissing me," he lifted his arm, mockery dripping from his voice, "my disfigurement repulsed you."

Ivonne surged to her feet.

How can he think that?

She shook her head, her hair swirling about her shoulders and back. "No, you have it wrong. I'm not disgusted. I would never—"

"Spare me your feeble excuses." He laughed, a cynical bark of amusement. "I'm well aware of how females react to my wounds, and your expression says much."

His hostile gaze cut a wide swath across her vulnerable heart and sliced it open, leaving a gaping wound. Hands lifted palm upward in entreaty, she moved toward him.

He took a single step backward. Detached regard

replaced the heated glimmer his eyes had held moments before.

The look froze her in place.

He despises me.

The knife twisted deeper into her bleeding heart.

Somehow, she must make him understand. "My tears are for what you've lost, Falcon, for what you'll never have."

He gathered his coat and then draped it across his unmarred arm.

"Or," with bored nonchalance, he yawned behind his misshapen hand, "do you weep for what *you'll* never have?"

She jerked her head as if he'd slapped her.

"You've proved yourself wholly disappointing." After sketching a mocking bow, Falcon presented his back and strode from the room.

Ivonne stared at the vacant doorway. The pre-dawn chill roused her from her stupor as the library clock tolled the hour of three. She blinked several times in an attempt to gather her scattered wits. The agony of her shattered heart hurt far worse than the breaks in her legs ever had. Shivering, she hugged her shoulders.

Had Falcon kissed her to determine if she would measure up? And found her wanting?

Ivonne furrowed her brow. No, he wouldn't do that. Would he?

She cast a glance toward the room's entrance.

Perhaps the old Falcon wouldn't have, but this new one ...?

Ivonne didn't know what him capable of anymore. She took a shaky breath, fearing he had toyed with her. The notion sickened her. He'd become callous. His words, though softly spoken, lanced deeper than a short sword. She'd been ten times a fool to harbor any hope he regarded her with anything more than ... what?

Not brotherly affection, for certain. Their kiss proved that beyond measure. Inexperienced she might be, but he'd been every bit as engaged as she.

Or perhaps not.

Retying the sash at her waist, she curled her toes against the numbing cold permeating her feet and rising to her calves.

Rogues faked ardor and affection.

Mother had warned her of that very thing when, motivated by lust for her sizable settlement, particularly unsavory gentlemen had begun to pay Ivonne uncommon attention. Her heart rebelled at likening Falcon to that lot, yet he had refused to even listen to her explanation.

He called me wholly disappointing.

One at a time, Ivonne blew out Falcon's candelabrum's tapers. In the increasing gloom, doubt niggled. Had his wounds and the savagery of warfare made him angry and bitter? It appeared he'd changed much.

What was the exact nature of the damage to his male parts? She wasn't supposed to know of such things, but as she matured, ladies became less cautious about what they whispered in her presence. She'd had quite an education these past two Seasons about men's *Man Thomas's* and *whirligigs.*

Nonetheless, she could claim more ignorance than knowledge.

Did men feel desire and have urges if that region was impaired? There wasn't anyone she could ask.

Mother would faint dead away, and Dawson, Ivonne's aged abigail, would expire from apoplexy. To ask Father or Allen was unthinkable.

I say, Allen, Father, would you please explain to me precisely what losing one's manhood entails? Don't concern yourself with my delicate sensibilities. I assure you, I want to know every last detail.

She almost giggled, imagining their appalled reactions.

Perhaps Falcon had only lost the ability to father children. Was he intact?

Did it matter?

Her gaze drifted to the piano bench, where moments before she'd experienced her greatest joy.

No, it didn't matter. Not to her.

Yes, she desired children, desperately. However, she wanted Falcon more. Besides, she'd already determined before he returned that spinsterhood was her fate. There'd be no brood of chubby-cheeked toddlers hanging on her skirts.

Ivonne smiled sadly and retrieved her candleholder.

She loved Falcon—deeply, gut-wrenchingly, beyond everything loved him. Loved him enough that she would marry him despite his disfigurement.

If he'd have her. Though truthfully, she stood a greater chance of weeping tears of gold.

A lifetime without him would be far bleaker than one deprived of children. Besides, waifs and orphans aplenty wandered London's streets, desperate for a good home.

She released a hefty sigh. It mattered not.

Such imaginations were the stuff of nonsensical fairy-tales. She inhaled a tremulous breath. Hadn't his reaction, his harsh words, proved his position?

He found her lacking.

Tears coursed down her cheeks. Ivonne made no attempt to wipe her face as she plodded toward her bedchamber.

This time, she did weep for what she would never have.

Her tears were short-lived, however. Before she reached the top riser of the curved stairway, her sorrow transformed to ire. Fury like none she had ever known burgeoned within her.

Enough of men acting like I am beneath their touch.

Falcon wasn't that different from Captain Kirkpatrick and the other gentlemen in that regard. He ... they believed her drab, undesirable, *disappointing.*

Well, this dowdy mouse was about to make a bold transformation.

Newfound determination in her step, Ivonne marched to her chamber. No more being made sport of and pitied for her ordinary appearance. She was about to set London on its ear.

"Just you wait, gentlemen."

10

"Miss Ivonne, wake up." Dawson prodded Ivonne's shoulder with a bony finger.

Ivonne groaned and forced her eyelids open. She raised a hand to her forehead and blinked away the grittiness in her eyes from too much crying and not enough sleep. Memories of last night and Falcon descended, the burden of their dual yoke weighing heavily upon her.

Seizing the jonquil velvet bed curtains, the maid swept them to either bedpost. "His lordship and her ladyship wish you to meet them in the study."

Plucking at the embroidered counterpane topping her bed, Ivonne sighed. She longed to crawl beneath the silk coverlet and ignore her parents' summons. She could claim to be indisposed. Truth to tell, she did feel rather awful. ... Until she remembered the plan she concocted last night. She barely refrained from an unladylike snicker and rubbing her hands together in glee.

Moments later, Dawson threw open the heavy draperies. Sunlight blazed into the chamber, revealing a breakfast tray atop a dainty table situated before the balcony. A chemise, stockings, and a mint green morning dress trimmed in ecru lace lay draped across a rosewood fainting couch.

"I let you sleep as long as I could." Dawson grinned, revealing her slightly crooked front teeth. "You didn't stir a jot, even when I cleaned the grate."

Ivonne yawned and sat up. She attempted to smooth her tangled hair. She ought to have plaited the mane before retiring. "I couldn't sleep last night. The hour was after five when I finally dozed off."

She gestured in the direction of the tray and gown. "I see you've been busy this morning."

"Morning?" Dawson chuckled, deep wrinkles etching her face. She pointed to the boudoir clock.

"Not for an hour."

"It's after one?" Ivonne stared in disbelief. She leaped from the bed, and then winced, laying a hand to her head. Pain thrummed behind her eyes. "I never sleep this late. What time am I to meet my parents?"

"Two o'clock. Sharp." Dawson tucked a stray grayish-blonde strand of hair into her cap. "The master's exact words."

After a hasty washing and slightly less swift toilette, Ivonne gulped down two bites of toast and a swallow of tepid tea. She shot the clock a hurried glance. Three minutes to make the study. Though normally good-natured, Father didn't abide tardiness.

So much for putting the scheme she'd hatched into action today, dash it all. With a little wave to Dawson, Ivonne hustled from her bedchamber. On second thought, this was better. It gave her more time to plot.

The first item on the agenda?

A secret meeting with her notorious second cousin, Emilia Leighton. A well-known demirep, Emmy seemed the perfect person to help Ivonne accomplish the task she'd set herself: transforming into an alluring creature no man could resist, least of all a golden-haired Greek god.

Not that I would have him after last night.

A wave of trepidation swept Ivonne. God help her if caught with Emmy. Turning a corner, Ivonne lifted her skirt and picked up her pace. Emmy wasn't received by anyone in the family these days. Although if the *on dit* could be believed, she was most popular with the demimonde and gaming hell set.

Ivonne had frequently heard Emmy's name whispered at elite gatherings. Usually spiteful remarks made behind fans by matrons long past their prime or on-the-shelf ladies, their voices shrill with envy.

Breathless from rushing down two corridors and the flight of stairs, Ivonne paused outside Father's study. The black walnut door stood closed.

People murmured within, their voices a muted drone through the thick wood.

Taking a deep breath, she smoothed her skirt and squared her shoulders. With newfound resolve, she rapped twice. The carved door swung open before she lowered her hand. The study smelled of leather, tobacco, and Father's cologne. She breathed in the familiar, comforting essence.

"Hullo, Sleeping Beauty. I've never known you to slumber this late." Allen grinned and leaned down to peck her cheek. Stepping back, he examined her. "I must say, the rest did you good. You look exquisite today, sister."

Pleased as Punch by the compliment, Ivonne placed her hand on his arm.

From his contrived messy hairstyle to his pristine knotted cravat and gleaming Hessians, Allen epitomized current fashion. Even the tobacco brown jacket he wore matched his hair to perfection and deepened his eyes to malachite. The next Viscount Wimpleton could claim exceptional looks, as could Mother and Father.

Ivonne, alone, possessed a sparrow's drab plumage.

She smiled inwardly. Not for long although she'd held no aspirations of ever nearing Mother's beauty. Raven haired and possessing the same unusual green eyes as Allen, Mother—at five and forty—outshone most women half her age. Today, the soft coral and peach gown complemented her flawless skin's youthful glow.

Father cut quite a handsome figure as well. Tall and slender, he boasted a full head of chestnut hair sprinkled with gray at the sideburns. At two and fifty, his striking, almost foreign features garnered much attention from moon-eyed females. He claimed a notorious sheik lurked in the family tree several generations back.

Now that would be a tale worth hearing.

After closing the heavy door, Allen guided Ivonne further into the room. "What, were you prowling about last night instead of sleeping? Or did sweet dreams of handsome beaus keep you abed?"

Her heart lurched for a panicked instant, and she searched his humor-filled eyes. He couldn't possibly know about her pre-dawn encounter with Falcon.

Allen winked.

She smiled as much in relief as at his teasing banter. No, he didn't know.

"I assumed you'd be hard-pressed to sleep, too,

brother dearest." She grinned and whispered, "I saw the charming Miss Kingsley last night."

A guarded expression entered Allen's eyes, although his smile didn't falter. "As did I, minx. I shall see her today too. She agreed to become my wife last night."

Miss Rossington was out of the picture, thank God.

Ivonne's smile widened, and she hugged him. "Now that is most welcome news."

Miss Rossington must have caught wind of the betrothal.

I wish I'd been present to witness that.

It explained her peevish behavior toward Miss Kingsley in the retiring room.

"Come along, you two." Father pocketed his watch. "Allen and I have a four o'clock appointment at White's. One I'm not looking forward to, I might add."

Ivonne considered him. He appeared a trifle tense, and his attention repeatedly fell to the papers scattered atop his desk. Most irregular. Father typically kept his desk neat and tidy.

THE LIEUTENANT AND THE LADY

Mother, seated on a cherry-red damask sofa, smiled and held out her arms. "Darling, that gown does remarkable things to your skin, and your eyes are a spectacular shade of green today."

Ivonne breathed an iota easier.

She'd been afraid her mother would detect traces of last night's waterworks. Cosmetics hid the evidence quite nicely, and Ivonne also credited them for the improvement in her appearance. The transformation the light touch of rice power and lip rouge achieved proved remarkable, the boost in her self-assurance, nothing short of astonishing.

Mother twisted to catch Father's attention. "Don't you agree, Walter?"

Father glanced to his wife then squinted at Ivonne.

"Yes, you're quite right, my dear." He smiled, his eyes crinkling at the corners. "Ivonne, you do look exceptionally lovely this afternoon."

She couldn't contain her wide grin.

Precisely what she'd hoped for. Emmy could advise her on what other artifices Ivonne should purchase. She quite liked feeling attractive. She intended to utilize the cosmetics, and anything else her cousin recommended, on a daily basis.

She launched a silent prayer heavenward.

Let the gentlemen find my appearance pleasing as well.

Particularly one gentleman she sought to make jealous.

Now, if only I could learn to flirt.

After embracing her mother, Ivonne took a seat on the sofa.

Allen lounged against the desk, his countenance gone somber. He toed the edge of the Oriental carpet, seemingly distracted.

Ivonne met everyone's gazes in turn. Shifting on the settee, she faced her mother. "You wished to see me?"

"Dear, an upset occurred last night." Mother gave her a brittle smile.

Drat, drat, drat.

Ivonne dug her fingernails into the sofa's piping.

Here we go.

What had Captain Kirkpatrick said? She itched to

box his ears, the smelly tattlemonger.

Mother paused and looked to Father. A pinched expression wrinkled her forehead.

He inclined his head.

"To do with Luxmoore's father," Mother said.

Ivonne relaxed her grip. This wasn't about the captain. Or the events in the arbor or on the terrace. "Nothing serious, I pray. Is everything well today?"

"No, no, not at all, I'm afraid." Father sighed and tapped his pipe. He fingered the bowl. "His father died ... er ... unexpectedly last night. Poor Luxmoore learned of the tragedy while at our ball."

"That's awful." Ivonne's eyes welled with tears. Lord Luxmoore had always been unfailingly kind to her, and he had a delightful sense of humor.

Allen straightened and rubbed his forehead. "I've given my word we'll not discuss the misfortune with anyone outside of this house except Faulkenhurst."

Falcon? Where was he today, anyway? Had he departed for Suttoncliffe already? A surge of hurt seized her. She shrugged inwardly. So much the better for her plan to succeed. What he did was of no importance to her.

Liar.

Ivonne's stomach growled and then rumbled again, much louder. She pressed a hand to her complaining middle. Except for those bites of cold toast in her room earlier, she'd eaten nothing since snaring two Shrewsbury biscuits from the kitchen yesterday afternoon.

"I shall certainly keep Luxmoore's confidence." She rose partway. "If that's all, I am rather famished."

Cook usually had a tasty treat or two, fresh from the oven. Ivonne could almost taste the warm seedcake, or maybe there'd be fresh maid of honor tarts.

Father raised his hand. "No, my dear, that's not all."

"Oh." Ivonne dropped fully onto the sofa once more. What else was there? She searched her parents' faces before settling on Allen's.

His focus remained riveted on the carpet as he tormented the fringed edge with his boot.

"There's something else?" She reluctantly forced the question past her lips.

An uncomfortable, pregnant pause followed. Her family looked at each other before their troubled gazes settled on her.

Dash it all.

So much for avoiding the Captain Kirkpatrick bumblebroth. Best to get it done with.

Ivonne stared at her hands clenched atop her lap. Her fingertips gleamed white.

"I'm sorry I ventured onto the terrace alone." She scanned their strained faces again. "I wouldn't have had I known Captain Kirkpatrick had arrived. He wasn't invited, and I didn't expect him to be so brazen as to come with—"

Father shushed her with a casual wave of his hand. "That wasn't wise of you, but that's not the issue we need to address."

"Walter, must we? There's no other recourse? You're sure?" Mother's eyes glimmered with tears, and her chin quivered.

Alarm seared Ivonne.

Mother didn't cry in front of others.

Ivonne threw Allen a desperate look.

He stared at the floor, his mouth pressed into a grim ribbon.

Whatever was wrong?

Giving one curt nod, Father set down his pipe. "Ivonne, everyone at the ball last night—and by now, half of London—believes you are newly betrothed."

"Is that what this is about?" She released a relieved laugh. "Well, I'm not. We'll just have to refute that ludicrous chitchat."

Chuckling, she flattened her palms on her knees, easing the stiffness from her numb fingers. "*Le bon ton* does love to make a hullabaloo out of nothing."

"It's not as simple as that, Ivy." Allen crouched before her. He took her hands in his, giving them a squeeze. "You see, not only did Captain Kirkpatrick fuel that preposterous rumor, word of your *good news* reached Prinny."

Her breath left her in a rush, and Ivonne gaped at her brother. "Prinny? The Prince Regent?"

Who else, goosecap?

She swallowed, not liking the direction this conversation headed. "What has he to do with this farce?"

Allen squeezed her hands again. "Seems he's a particular friend of the Duke of Petheringstone, and that stinking lickspittle is as tight as a tick on a hog's arse with Kirkpatrick."

"Mind your tongue, Allen." Mother dabbed at her eyes with an embroidered handkerchief. She wrinkled her nose the merest bit. "Though it's true, Petheringstone has no more fondness for cleanliness than the captain."

Why are they blathering on about bathing habits?

Ivonne slanted her head to meet Father's gaze. "I don't understand how or why the prince is involved."

Father lifted an elaborate gold-trimmed, beribboned document clearly bearing the Regent's insignia. "The prince has demanded an introduction to the groom, and Prinny's announced he'll attend the wedding."

"Pardon?" Ivonne yanked her hands from Allen's. "You cannot be serious. The Regent hasn't spoken more than a dozen words to me since I was presented at court."

All pretense of calmness splintered to pieces.

Pressing her fingers to her temples, she tried to lessen the sudden pounding in her head. She darted a frantic glance to her father. "And I don't recall Father being a particular favorite of his either."

Unable to sit a moment longer, Ivonne surged to her feet.

"Why would he insist on attending my wedding?" She pointed at her chest before flapping her hand in the air. "An imaginary wedding at that?"

Tears pricked her eyelids and clogged her throat.

Father came round from behind his desk. Wrapping her in his embrace, he held her head against his chest and awkwardly patted her back.

"I'm afraid Petheringstone is an old enemy. I believe he suspects there's no groom and hopes to get us—your mother and I—deep in suds with His Highness."

Mother stood and touched Ivonne's shoulder. "Petheringstone never forgave your father for winning my hand in marriage."

"That's true." Father's voice rumbled deep in his chest as if he struggled with his emotions. "But more on point, he never forgave me for besting him in the duel we fought over you."

"Duel?" Allen and Ivonne chimed as one.

Father sighed before kissing the top of Ivonne's head. "Yes. He fired before the count finished. By the grace of God, he only nicked my shoulder."

"A drunken one-eyed goat herder has better aim than Petheringstone." Mother gazed at Father with admiration.

"True, the man's always been a wretched shot, though his skill with a blade is far worse." Father took a step away from Ivonne. "I had no desire to kill the blackguard, so I shot him in the foot, thinking the leather of his boot offered him some protection. He's been lame since."

"Some jealous cawker gets to dictate my future?" Ivonne couldn't keep the scorn from her voice.

Mother grasped Ivonne's shoulder, turning her until she faced her mother. "I'm sorry, darling. There's no help for it. The duke, much like Captain Kirkpatrick, is a man obsessed."

Cupping Ivonne's face, her mother attempted a

brave smile that better resembled a watery grimace.

"Petheringstone has the prince's ear and his favor. The Regent won't be dissuaded. That," Mother pointed to the oval desk where the document lay, "is, in effect, a royal decree."

"This is utterly ridiculous," Ivonne protested. "Who does he think he is, meddling in our private affairs? This is 1818, for pity's sake."

Allen slapped his thigh, his expression fierce. "Once he gets a notion in his pickled head, there's no changing his mind. His disfavor isn't something anyone wants to be at the receiving end of, I assure you."

He met Father's troubled gaze. "I'm certain you recollect what happened to Lord Forester when he ignored His Highness's *suggestion* that the baron ought to wed Mrs. Ellington."

"Mrs. Ellington?" Ivonne didn't recall her. And, come to think of it, she hadn't seen the baron at all this Season. "Who is Mrs. Ellington?"

Allen fumbled in pouring himself a glass of sherry and splashed a few droplets on the rosewood cabinet. "One of Prinny's ... ah ..."

"Mistresses who found herself in the family way." Pink tinted Mother's high cheekbones.

Ivonne fought the urge to roll her eyes skyward. For heaven's sake, they acted like she had no idea such indiscretions occurred. Half the *ton* engaged in dalliances.

Father nodded and pinched the bridge of his nose. "Ruined the poor man and his family. Last I heard, to keep a roof above his two sisters' and invalid mother's heads, Forester married another of Prinny's cast-offs."

Bother, blast, and damnation! Surely this is a terrible nightmare, and I'll awaken any moment.

Father returned to his chair behind the cumbersome mahogany partners' desk. Frowning, he read the letter from the prince again. He sighed and, apparently defeated, slouched against the leather. He gazed at her, his eyes dark with regret.

"Ivonne, I'm afraid we're at *point non plus*." His voice caught as he spoke. "You'll have to pick a suitor to bring up to scratch. If you don't, I will."

She gasped and clutched Mother's clammy hand.

"The wedding is two months from this Friday."

Father tapped the paper, his voice gaining strength. "Prinny expects to meet the groom within a fortnight."

11

That same day, across Town

Eyes narrowed, Chance stared at Samuel Tobbins. Assistant to Franklin Belamont, Chance's solicitor, Tobbins wiped his forehead with his limp handkerchief for the fourth time. The diminutive fellow perspired to such a degree, Chance half expected him to slosh when he walked.

"I assure you, your file hasn't been misplaced." The man flitted about the office like a disoriented moth, searching for the missing folder.

Arms crossed, Chance arched a brow.

"Where are they?" Tobbins bent to peer beneath a haphazard pile of papers atop an otherwise organized desk. Clicking his tongue, he scampered to another stack of files and began flipping through them. "Where in the world are they?"

"You mean to tell me you don't believe *any* of my correspondence or papers are here?" Chance gestured round the tidy office. "You think, perhaps, they've been forwarded to Suttoncliffe? The entire six years' worth?"

This was what came of having the same solicitor as Father and Thad.

"I'm sorry, Mr. Faulkenhurst, but yes." Nodding his balding head, Tobbins pushed his spectacles up his reedy nose. "I'm afraid that must be the case, for I cannot find a single document of yours."

He wrung his hands together, his watery hazel eyes huge and worried. "I expect Mr. Belamont's return from Rochester any day now, certainly not upward of a week. He can set you straight on the matter, I'm sure."

Tobbins riffled through another pile of papers on a shelf behind the solicitor's desk.

"Aha," he exclaimed holding up a letter and practically dancing with glee. One would have thought he'd found a large banknote from his enthusiastic reaction. "Here's a letter for you."

He scuttled to where Chance sat. With the aplomb of a royal courtier, he presented the missive.

After breaking the seal, Chance scanned the short correspondence.

Exasperated by Chance's failure to speedily sign the marriage agreement—for God's sake, what did Lambert expect? Chance had been in India—his lordship had foisted his daughter off on another poor sot.

Chance examined the letter's date. April.

All his worry had been for naught.

He refolded the paper and slid it into his coat pocket. A wry grin crept across his face.

One monumental obstacle out of the way.

"Good news, sir?" Tobbins waited, an expectant look on his face.

"Exceedingly good news."

Chance shifted in the uncomfortable, smallish chair, far more appropriate for waiting in the hall than a lengthy meeting in a solicitor's office. His missing fingers picked today to ache unbearably. Every twinge reminded him of last night and the pleasure of playing the piano with Ivy.

And kissing and caressing her.

That kiss. God help him, but he'd been hard put to keep from ravishing her right there in the drawing room while her parents and brother slept above. Her response had been a precious and unexpected gift. He'd never lost control that completely or quickly. Ivy was like nectar to his parched soul, balm to his wounded spirit.

Then she'd wept, and the vile truth hit him with the impact of a cannonball. He'd tasted her tears, the salt bitter on his lips. More rancorous was the despair that seized his heart, destroying the fragile remnant of hope buried there.

She couldn't overlook his disfigurement.

Anger and hurt had overwhelmed his good sense, and he'd been cruel.

Last night had been a calamity, and except for learning the proposed marriage agreement with Mrs. Washburn was cancelled, little about this day had gone right either. He sighed and stood.

"The moment Belamont returns, please tell him I require an immediate appointment."

"I shall, sir, you can be certain." His relief tangible, Tobbins attempted a smile and opened the office door.

"I'm staying at Viscount Wimpleton's residence. Please send word to me there." Chance slapped his hat on his head. He didn't have a card to offer with the Wimpletons' address on it. "Do you know the place?"

"Oh, yes, of course." Tobbins continued to bob his head, reminding Chance of a nervous quail. "Berkeley Square in Mayfair."

With a curt nod, Chance made his escape. Lost in thought, he set a brisk pace for several blocks. He crossed the street, dodging a landau stuffed with giggling misses. He recognized two of the fivesome, the Dundercroft sisters. He'd made their acquaintance last night.

Poised beneath her lacy parasol, the younger smiled and waved to him.

The elder swatted her sister's hand and, after sending him a glare of reproach, scolded her sister soundly.

It seemed one of the Misses Dundercroft had taken distinct exception to him and the other a definite fancy. He executed a mocking half-bow and allowed a droll smile to tilt his mouth.

A young Corinthian astride a magnificent Arabian trotted by.

Chance needed to purchase a horse—a serviceable, though not expensive, stepper. Perchance Allen could be imposed upon to accompany him to Tattersall's tomorrow.

And perhaps he had an acquaintance who, for a nominal fee, could investigate Robinson and locate his place of business in London for Chance as well. He must at least attempt to regain his lost funds. He blew out a long puff of air. He had about as much chance of that as a jellyfish surviving in the Great Thar Desert.

Rounding a corner, he strode in the direction of St. James Street. He'd sold his lieutenant's commission an hour ago and, after depositing the nominal amount in the bank, had continued on to his solicitor's. Chance had wanted to be on his way to Suttoncliffe the day after tomorrow. By Sunday at the latest, but Belamont's absence complicated matters.

Perhaps Chance wouldn't remain in Town after all. He'd waited this long to speak with the man. Another week seemed insignificant. Besides, his curiosity was aroused. Were his papers and correspondences at Suttoncliffe Hall?

If not, where the devil were they?

He flicked his pocket watch open. Quarter to five. He was late, but White's was only a couple of blocks farther along this street, and Allen would linger. After all these years apart, their friendship hadn't waned. Nevertheless, Chance increased his pace.

The morning and afternoon hadn't gone as anticipated.

First, he'd overslept. No surprise there.

After seeing Ivy partially dishabille, a seductress in that clingy purple gown and robe, he'd given in to the urge to kiss her senseless—something he had yearned to do for years. He didn't regret kissing her. Never had a woman's lips tasted sweeter, made all the more so by his unprofessed love for her.

Love he didn't have the right to proclaim.

Had her tears been born of pity and disgust?

Last night, that notion fueled the anger he'd kept repressed regarding the war, his injuries, his lost fortune, and his father's meddling. His stride slowed. He'd believed Ivy different than the other women who scorned him because of his disfigurements. Her joy upon seeing him in the arbor had given him momentary hope. Her responses to his kisses had fueled his corkbrained optimism further.

Lying awake in the plush, oversized bed, the most comfortable place he'd rested in six years, his thoughts repeatedly turned to her asleep in her room. Why had she come below stairs in the first place? She'd seemed as eager to see him as he'd been to see her. She had enjoyed their kiss too.

Now they were estranged, and he had only himself to blame.

Chance couldn't bear to have her angry with him. If she refused to speak to him ever again, he wouldn't blame her. He'd been an ass of the worst sort. He must make amends and apologize to her before he left for

Suttoncliffe.

Actually, his time in England might very well be limited altogether.

Something Sethwick's viscountess had said at the ball last night piqued Chance's interest. Her late father had built a shipping conglomeration, which she now owned. Stapleton Shipping and Supplies had offices around the world, including Boston, Massachusetts. Chance was of a mind to inquire if any positions were available in the American offices.

Seeing Ivy again had made him realize why he'd left England the first time; aside from needing a fortune to entice her father that is.

To have the object of his affection this close, yet always unattainable was unbearable. The bowels of Hades boasted lavish comfort in comparison to the torment. He wasn't confident he wouldn't blurt his feelings to her at some point.

Her repugnance toward his injury was painful enough to tolerate, but that she wasn't ever allowed to accept his love, even more so. Lord Wimpleton had made it clear that Chance wasn't worthy of his daughter.

No, that was unfair.

Increasing his pace, Chance switched his cane to his other hand then immediately transferred the staff back again. Blast, so easy to forget he wasn't whole anymore.

Wimpleton hadn't refused his proposal outright. The viscount had told him to return when he had something to offer. Chance had failed in that respect.

If Ivy had even hinted last night that she returned his regard with the same fervency he felt toward her, he would ignore his circumstances and ask her to marry him. She was of age, and Wimpleton didn't seem the sort to disown his daughter for marrying without permission. But was she the sort of woman to openly defy her father?

Her response to Chance in the drawing room gave him little confidence Ivy was smitten enough to cause a scandal. Besides, she'd lived a life of luxury and privilege. While not a spoilt *tonnish* damsel, she would find the meager existence he could provide more than difficult. She deserved the finest life had to offer, and he couldn't give her that.

He wasn't the sort to tap into her marriage settlement to make ends meet, either. Those funds belonged to her, to do with as she wished. So, he found himself precisely where he'd begun six years ago.

In love and without a means of providing for her.

Only a fool believed love was enough to make a go of it.

Oh, but he would play the fool a thousand times over for one chance to make Ivy his. He'd gamble his life for that opportunity and worry about how to care for her afterward. He would bury his pride and accept any employment offer that came his way.

Chance smiled as a ragged urchin raced down the street, a scraggly black dog at his bare heels.

He didn't understand Ivy's lack of suitable beaus. He might not be able to claim her, but, as long as he had a breath in his body, she'd never settle for the likes of that piss maker, Kirkpatrick.

Ever.

White's came into view. The Duke of Argyll and Lord Worcester sat in the bow window, no doubt making ludicrous wagers on everything from where a bird dropping might land on the pavement to whether a passerby might sneeze or fart.

Chance supposed those with deep pockets didn't think twice about wasting funds. He couldn't recall the last time he'd wagered on anything, unless he counted the investment fiasco with Robinson. Men with pockets to let, such as he, didn't toss coin about like cracked corn to chickens.

He entered the exclusive establishment, seeking Allen and the others who'd been apprised of Luxmoore's calamity. Sorrow for his long-time friend gripped him.

Where were they?

He perused the interior, spying the group at a table in a secluded corner. Heads bent near, as if they didn't want their conversation overheard, only Harcourt, Sethwick, and Allen conferred at the table. Two chairs sat empty, Lord Wimpleton evidently having departed already.

Chance closed the distance with long strides, suddenly famished and eager to see his friends. By God, he'd missed them these past years. Smiling, he opened his mouth in greeting.

Allen's words stopped him cold.

"Prinny's adamant. Thanks to Kirkpatrick's meddling, my sister must produce a groom within a fortnight and wed within two months."

Bloody hell.

12

Seated on the arbor bench, Ivonne kicked at a small pebble. It pinged against the lattice then rolled beneath some foliage. After the devastating announcement in Father's study, she'd flown straight here, to her sanctuary.

Damnation.

Pick a suitor to marry. Just like that. As if she selected a new bonnet or a pair of slippers instead of a husband. How could the Regent make such an absurd demand? Interfering fat toad. This wasn't the Dark Ages, for pity's sake.

Produce a betrothed and invite me to the wedding or ... or ... off with your head.

Suffocating waves of dread choked Ivonne. She

closed her eyes, fearing she would swoon.

Dear God. She must pick a man to wed, or Father would pick for her. This was real, not some horrid nightmare she'd awaken from. What was she to do? She couldn't marry any of the men interested in her. She just couldn't.

She stifled a panicked sob. Pressing her fists to her eyes, she refused to let the tears come. Crying, what a wretched waste of time and energy.

Think, Ivonne. There must be another alternative.

Did her parents understand the dismal selection available?

Ivonne mentally catalogued her choices: two decrepit old scallywags who smelt of camphor and four fortune-seeking rakehells, each of whom possessed a title and likely carried the clap. And—she shuddered, sickened at the thought—wealthy, fetid Captain Kirkpatrick.

Never him. Not while the sun rises.

Arms folded, she sagged further into the bench's carved back. Sorry lot, each and every one. The corpulent prince could starve himself before she ever agreed to marry any of them.

Several black ants maneuvered past her slipper carrying a dead bee.

She couldn't believe her parents would force her to marry to satisfy the Regent's whim. They'd more mettle than that.

Why acquiesce so easily? It wasn't like them at all.

Shoulders hunched, she sighed. This wasn't simply about her. The Sovereign, much like an intractable child, had a malicious streak when opposed. A chill swept her. She hadn't a fool's doubt he would destroy her family, if not financially then socially. They'd be ostracized. She fiddled with the lace along her gown's neckline. Did Prinny have the power to strip Father of his viscountcy?

What would become of her family then?

A pair of beautiful grayish-blue eyes invaded her musings. If only Falcon were a beau, her decision would be oh-so-easy.

"I ought to propose to Falcon. Wouldn't that set the prince and his cronies on their ears?" She scuffed her shoes on the leaf-littered ground. A black-capped coal tit chirped nearby, as if in agreement.

Ivonne suddenly straightened. The idea wasn't that farfetched. In fact, the notion possessed a great deal of merit. Shoving aside her hurt and irritation about Falcon's behavior last night, she took a mental inventory.

His lineage was impeccable, and his honor equally so. He didn't possess a fortune or a title, but then, how many second sons did? Her marriage settlement, if managed wisely, would allow them a lifetime of relative ease. Nothing lavish, but modest comfort, which suited her fine, truth to tell.

They were compatible, already good friends, and he'd enjoyed their intimate encounter. At least she thought he had. That meant he found her somewhat appealing, didn't it?

She bit her lip. Unless last night destroyed any chance of him wanting her.

He'd been brutal—more angry and hurtful than she'd ever known him to be.

Her heart gave a painful twinge. Well then, she'd have to change his mind. She had wanted to marry him for as long as she could remember. Only she hadn't anticipated being the party to initiate the proposal. It just wasn't done in the finer circles.

The coal tit hopped onto a branch and cocked its head, staring at her with tiny ebony eyes. Ivonne chuckled. "What's wrong with a woman proposing to a man, I ask you, my petite friend? Female birds select their mates all the time."

Did she dare?

Why not?

What did she have to lose?

Nothing.

And she had everything to gain if Falcon should agree.

It wasn't likely he courted anyone else, as yet. He'd only been in England a few days.

Ivonne would rather risk humiliation by setting her cap for him than settle on one of the other men interested in her, or rather, interested in her marriage portion. If Falcon refused her, it didn't much matter who she married. She would be miserable, thanks to the prince's meddling.

With Falcon, she could be happy. Ivonne had never been more certain of anything. And she could make him happy, too, given the chance.

She had bribed Burke, the new under footman, to take a note round to Emmy this morning. Ivonne prayed for a prompt response from her cousin. Originally, she intended to use her cousin's talents to prove to the pretentious *ton* that she could attract a great catch if Ivonne chose to. She hadn't been of a mind to lure suitors before last night's events. In fact, she'd done her best to repel them.

However, as of a few moments ago, her efforts centered on a single purpose—winning Falcon. She hadn't any time to lose if, in the next fortnight, she was to convince him to marry her. She wasn't sure how to go about wooing a man, but Emmy would know.

Her outlook much brighter, Ivonne smiled and glanced around the arbor. Last night she thought her life doomed when Falcon uttered those fateful words in the arbor. The Regent's dictate might have made it possible for her to have the one thing that mattered most.

Falcon.

Humming a jaunty tune, she strolled the footpath to the house. Head down, she plotted her tactics. She imagined and analyzed every possible situation. Mother must be informed of the need of an immediate shopping excursion, and a new hair style, perfume ... everything.

Yes, this dowdy bird was determined to shed her dull plumage and leg-shackle herself to a divine husband. One god-like former soldier who'd soon forget he had ever looked upon her as an annoying little sister.

Assembling a mental shopping list, Ivonne plowed full on into a firm male body. She stumbled, her lame leg giving way, and lost her balance. Strong arms encircled her and held her tight to a wide navy-clad chest.

Falcon. She recognized his cologne and the breadth of his shoulders. The urge to snuggle closer to him, wrap her arms around his neck and kiss his jaw overwhelmed her. Instead, she breathed in his scent, savoring his unique aroma.

Now was as good a time as any to set the snare.

Tipping her head upward, she offered what she

hoped was an enticing smile. "I was just thinking of you."

Surprise tempered with wariness flitted within his eyes. He stepped back, his hands grasping her upper arms. "Were you now?"

Was he still angry?

"Yes, actually." She nodded and peeked at him, and then, self-consciousness shrouding her, averted her gaze. "I was remembering last night."

Ivonne wanted to say *our kiss*, but she lost her nerve.

Peering at him through half-closed eyes made it deuced difficult to see anything clearly. How women managed to look sultry while doing so, she couldn't imagine. She wasn't about to bat her eyelashes like Miss Rossington did. Ivonne feared she'd appear to be having an apoplexy.

Bother. She had much to learn about womanly wiles and little time to acquire the skills necessary to obtain her husband of choice.

Cautious, Falcon eyed her, a hint of amusement creasing the corners of his blue eyes. "Last night?"

"Yes ... er ..." At her ineptitude, dual paths of heat flamed across her cheeks.

He crooked a brow, his mouth sliding into one of his lopsided, boyish grins, though he offered her no succor. He wasn't going to make this easy, was he?

Drawing a deep breath, Ivonne tried again.

"I enjoyed our time together last night. That is..." She fumbled to a stop.

He bent nearer and whispered, "Which part?"

The seductive cadence of his voice sent tiny delicious shivers skittering across her bare arms. She stared at his lips. She wanted him to kiss her again. Desperately.

A half-smile curving his lips, he regarded her steadily.

An exciting spark heated her womanly places. She'd wager her best bonnet he knew exactly what direction her thoughts had taken.

He focused on her mouth. "Yes, that kissing bit was rather nice, wasn't it?"

"Yes," she breathed.

His gaze glided over her, taking her measure from

slippers to hair, lingering the merest jot too long on her bosom to be considered polite. "You are lovely."

Three simple words sent her senses into a riotous dither. Warmth scorched her cheeks again, and her tongue refused to form an appropriate response. Had he forgotten his irritation of last evening, or had he decided to put it aside? It mattered not to her. This was the charming Falcon she remembered. The one she loved.

Tucking her hand into the bend of his elbow, he steered her in the terrace's direction. Her knees threatened to give out at his touch. What a ninny.

Compose yourself, Ivonne.

His forearm flexed beneath her fingers. "I sought you out to apologize for my behavior last night."

"There's no need—"

"Yes, there is." Falcon guided her to a scrolled metal bench in full view of the house's French windows. "Please, sit and indulge me for a moment."

Sinking onto the seat, she cast a surreptitious look at the manor. Dawson probably had her face pressed flat against the upper windowpanes while Mother peeked around the drawing room curtains and watched their every move. The last rays of the sun caressed the structure with their warm glow, making it impossible to discern if anyone did, indeed, spy upon them.

Hands folded in her lap, Ivonne faced him. Did he prefer demure, biddable women? She had no idea. She'd only been his friend until now. Before she bungled this wooing business beyond repair, she must meet with Emmy and discover what men desired.

Falcon sat upon the bench, a respectable distance between them this time. His buff doe-skins revealed long, muscled legs.

She covertly studied his groin, ignoring the telltale warmth suffusing her face once more. The bulge his pantaloons couldn't hide seemed similar to those of other men. Everything appeared as it should, at least to her inexperienced assessment.

He fidgeted with his watch fob, running the fingers of his intact hand along the fine silver chain. "Last night, I took advantage of you—"

"No, I—"

He put one finger on her lips. "Shh, let me finish."

She swallowed and clenched her fists to keep from tracing his finger with her tongue, or taking the entire thing into her mouth and sucking on it.

Where are these wanton ideas coming from?

He tossed a glance over his shoulder as if he, too, believed someone observed them. His sculptured mouth twitched. "I think we're being watched."

Ivonne giggled and leaned closer. "I'm sure of it. Too bad we don't dare give them something to gape at."

Staring straight ahead, he didn't respond. "I shouldn't have kissed you. I had no right. But more on point, I beg your forgiveness for accusing you of satisfying your curiosity with me, and then saying those other deplorable things."

He finished the last with a rush of words, as if he'd dreaded saying them.

Ivonne cocked her head, studying his profile. His remorse appeared genuine. Her pulse gave a little leap of hope. This made what she was about to suggest all the more feasible.

"Falcon." Jaw flexed, she pulled in a lengthy gulp

of air and delved for courage. She pinched her fingers together, striving for calmness. "I have something to ask you."

"There you two are. Mother said I'd find you out here somewhere."

Allen? Ivonne twisted to look behind her. He strode the distance to the bench. The curtain twitched in the drawing room. Mother?

Ivonne and Falcon sat in plain view.

Had Mother sent Allen after them? Whatever for?

"I received some news that will be of great interest to you, Falcon." Ankles crossed, Allen rested his left hip against the balustrade. A peculiar expression settled on his face. His gaze swung between her and Falcon. "Am I interrupting something?"

Yes, dear brother, you are. A proposal.

"No, not at all." Falcon shook his head.

Allen flashed Ivonne one of his devastating smiles. "Mother asked me to remind you it's time to dress for the Vanbroke's musicale."

Ivonne furrowed her forehead and laced her fingers. "After last night, I expected we'd cry off attending."

"No." Allen firmed his lips and straightened. "Father insists the entire family put in an appearance to curb the gossipmongers' wagging tongues."

Too late for that, she feared. She turned her attention to Falcon. Rising, she straightened her gown. "Are you joining us? Safety in numbers, you know."

She tried to make the question seem casual, not as if her very future depended upon him being by her side from this point forward. Curling her toes in her slippers, she struggled to calm her nerves. If she stuck to him like fuzz on a peach, she'd send a clear message to everyone.

She'd made her choice. He just didn't know it.

"No, I'm afraid not." Falcon slid Allen a significant look.

Allen's eyebrows formed a puzzled vee, yet he remained silent.

Returning his fob to its pocket, Falcon stood. "I've been invited to dine with the Sethwicks this evening."

His gaze lingered on Ivonne's face, as if trying to memorize her features. Or gauge her reaction?

She swallowed, suddenly not wanting to hear what he was about to say.

He stared at her intently. "Lady Sethwick has a position open in her American shipping offices that I'm interested in."

13

Back rigid, Chance held his breath, waiting for Ivy's reaction. A muscle ticked annoyingly at the corner of his eye, revealing his agitation. Much weighed on whether she wanted him to stay. Moments ago, sitting beside her, he'd been tempted to throw good sense to the wind and ask her to be his bride, propriety be hanged.

A soft gasp escaped her. "America?"

She darted Allen an anxious glance before returning her attention to Chance. Her eyes, an unusual pewter shade in the dusky light, widened in astonishment and glistened suspiciously.

Tears?

He revered her with his gaze.

Bronze highlights shimmered in her hair, and her skin, pale as pearls, glowed in the sun's fading rays.

He longed to tell her of her beauty with more than words. To take her in his arms and worship her with his lips and body, to whisper the words of adoration he didn't dare share.

"America?" she rasped again, her lips trembling. Shaking her head, she clapped a hand to her mouth, her curls and peridot earrings bouncing from the frenzied movement. Without another word, she whirled away and hastened to the house.

For the first time, Chance noticed her lopsided gait.

Allen chuckled softly and sent him a sidelong glance. "I'd say that answers the question of where her affections lie, my friend."

Chance had initiated a very candid conversation with Allen after overhearing the remark at White's about Prinny's ludicrous decree. The Wimpleton heir had been delighted when Chance revealed his love for Ivy. Allen promised to throw all his support behind Chance's attempt to win her hand.

If Lord Wimpleton once more denied Chance's request to marry her, wisdom dictated he have an alternate plan. He'd chosen America as that option.

"Yes, my unflappable sister is in a dither at the notion of you sailing off across the Atlantic to the wilds of America." He slapped Chance on the back.

Chance flinched, smothering a foul oath. "Bugger it. Have care for my injured arm, will you?"

"Sorry 'bout that." Allen grinned sheepishly. He jabbed his thumb in the direction Ivy had disappeared. "That wasn't the reaction of a disinterested woman. No, I'd say she's already smitten."

A cocky grin tilting his mouth, he stepped away and took Chance's measure. "I suppose you'll do for a brother-in-law."

Chance allowed himself a cautious smile. "Not so fast. There's your father to convince. He must be made to see that I'm the best choice Ivy has for happiness."

"You haven't seen the competition." Allen laughed and scratched his nose. "Trust me. Father, and Mother, especially, will be groveling at your feet in gratitude. They want my sister to be happy, which is why they haven't pushed her to marry before now."

He rested a hip on the bannister and gazed at the brilliant sunset.

"Truth be told, I'm rather surprised how easily Father conceded to Prinny's demand. I have no more desire to incur the Regent's wrath than anyone else, but Father didn't attempt to stall his royal rotundness."

Allen pulled on his earlobe, his countenance bewildered. "Wholly out of character for my sire, I assure you."

He swung his gaze to Chance, speculation in its green depths.

"It's almost as if he knew of your interest in my sister."

Chance gave a low laugh. "He did. I asked for her hand years ago. The viscount told me to make a request again when she was older, and I had something to offer her."

Allen's mouth fell open. He gaped at Chance.

"Devil it, you didn't. *He didn't.*" Allen turned to stare at the house. "That sly fox. He knows exactly what he's about."

His mouth skewed into an appreciative smirk, he shook his head. "He knows Ivonne's taken with you and won't accept another. Father's forcing your hand."

Chance wished he agreed with Allen's assessment of the situation. Truth be told, his friend's explanation seemed far too simple and fortuitous.

"Perhaps. However, I have my doubts." Straightening his waistcoat, Chance shifted toward the manor as well.

"I've been absent six years. People will find it peculiar that immediately upon my return to England, Ivy and I are betrothed. You know they'll ask why there wasn't a single hint or mention of an arrangement between us in all this time."

The sun sank lower on the pastel horizon. A cricket's buzzing chirrup rang nearby. He needed to be on his way soon, or he would be tardy for dinner. Not the way to impress a potential employer.

"How do you and your parents intend to explain other men courting your sister in my absence?" He rubbed his sore arm and then snorted. "Brows will raise and whispers will be tossed about, *if* I can somehow manage to get Wimpleton's approval."

"Oh, you'll get it all right," Allen assured him. "And don't worry about the courting. None of those sots ever paid her their formal addresses. A few unworthy curs sought her hand, but Father made it clear they should turn their attentions elsewhere."

A delighted chuckle escaped his friend.

"I'm willing to bet my best mare that Father regretted refusing you the moment he realized where my sister's affections lay. Mother probably deduced the truth and gave him a piece of her mind in the process. Women seem much more perceptive to that sort of thing."

Allen folded his arms, a pleased grin exposing his teeth.

"This is perfect, Falcon, don't you see? You claimed Ivonne was promised to another. Who else would know that except her affianced? Now that you're once again on British soil, we'll circulate the tale that an agreement was reached before you hied off to India."

"Why didn't we marry before I left?" Chance eyed

him doubtfully. "No one with an iota of sense would believe such fustian nonsense."

Allen shrugged. "Ivy was what? Fifteen when you left?"

"Almost sixteen."

"Definitely too young." Allen clasped both hands to his chest and, *sotto voce*, declared, "To leave her Mother's bosom and trot off to another continent at such a tender age? Unfathomable."

"You forget, Allen, I don't have anything to offer her. No title, no fortune, no lands. Not even an annual income."

Only the deepest, purest love a man ever had for a woman.

Would that be enough? For her, perhaps, but her father's approval mattered a great deal to Chance as well.

Allen faced him, all signs of silliness gone. His attention sank to Chance's mangled hand. "You love her. The rest shouldn't, and doesn't, matter."

A far-off glint entered his eyes. "I learned that the hard way."

Was love enough? Chance wasn't certain. A title, even attached to a blackguard or rogue, meant much to many of *le bon ton*. Perhaps the viscount numbered among those. Chance didn't know the man well enough to make that determination.

"Besides," Allen stretched his arms overhead. "I have news that might turn providence's favor your way. A few questions to the right chaps at Brooks's and White's, and I learned Robinson has a reputable establishment on Lombard Street."

"He's still conducting business?" Chance's gaze leaped to Allen, and he couldn't contain his surprise. "I thought him a thieving scapegrace long since gone."

A dove landed on the lawn. Watching them with its tiny black-button eyes, the bird poked around beneath a shrub.

"Apparently not." Allen brushed a speck of lint off his coat. "He's reputed to be honest and diligent. Several gentlemen I spoke to have engaged in financial endeavors with him."

He gave Chance a cocky grin. "Very lucrative dealings, I might add."

Ivonne tore to her room, barely making the threshold before the torrent of tears overflowed. She'd feared she would cast up her accounts or swoon when Falcon offhandedly mentioned his interest in leaving England. Collapsing on her bed, she sobbed until her throat and head ached.

Shoving her soggy pillow aside, she rolled over and heaved a gusty sigh.

America.

Falcon's announcement ripped her chest wide open, yanked out her fractured heart, and smashed it beneath the hooves of a thousand horses. Even breathing was a painful reminder of the annihilation of her pathetic dream.

She quirked her lips in self-castigation. When had she become so histrionic? Her gaze fell on a large basket sitting atop the chamber's small, square table. A crisp white sheet of paper peeked from between several wrapped bundles.

She frowned. What was that, and when had it arrived?

Emelia!

Ivonne leaped from the bed, swiping at her damp face with her fingers. She snatched the paper, taking a cursory glance at the basket's contents. After breaking the wax seal with her fingernail, she read the missive.

Her shoulders slumped in disappointment. A tight knot of defeat curled in her middle. Emmy wouldn't help. She'd sent along several fashion magazines, the name of an exclusive modiste, and a basket full of cosmetics, fripperies, and fallalls.

My darling Ivonne,

You've no need for my expertise. You are supremely lovely in your innocence, and any man who fails to recognize that truth isn't worthy of you. I sent along some new cosmetics ...

Ivonne wadded the note into a tiny ball. She tossed it in the fireplace as she dragged herself to the washstand. Eyes closed and fighting tears, she wiped her face with cool water from the pitcher. After changing into her nightgown, she climbed between the sheets. She lay staring at the canopy, her thoughts cavorting about in her mind.

No help from Emmy.

Falcon plans to leave England.

I must produce a groom in two weeks.

All is lost.

Dawson tiptoed into the chamber, her thin face etched with worry. Her astute gaze took in the basket, crumpled paper, and garments heaped upon the floor. "Can I get you anything?"

"Would you please tell Mother I'm indisposed?" Ivonne turned onto her side, tucking a hand beneath her pillow.

"Of course. I'll bring you some mint tea and toast too."

Dawson padded from the room, no doubt already aware of the reason for Ivonne's distress. Servants knew every tidbit, though how they came by the tattle was baffling, if not downright eerie at times.

Several moments later, two raps sounded at the door. Mother glided into the chamber without waiting for Ivonne to bid her enter.

"Darling, you're not well?" As she took in Ivonne's appearance, her mother's face creased with concern. "You're pale as the moon. Is it your stomach? A headache? Your leg?"

"No, none of those ail me." Ivonne shut her eyes lest her mother see the anguish that no doubt resided there.

Mother laid her cool hand on Ivonne's brow. "No fever, but you look entirely done in."

Ivonne released a shaky breath and opened her eyes.

"You've been crying." Her mother's brow furrowed into a frown. She sat upon the edge of the bed and smoothed Ivonne's hair. "I'm terribly sorry, my dear. This betrothal business has been too much for you."

After tucking the counterpane around Ivonne's shoulders, Mother kissed Ivonne's forehead. "I'll send our regrets to the Vanbrokes at once."

"No, Mother. You and Father should go. Perhaps your presence will help alleviate some of the chatter."

Ivonne didn't believe it for a minute. When the *ton* sank its talons into a juicy bit of gossip, no hope for redemption remained. Vultures on carrion, they delighted in everything foul and putrid.

Her mother shook her head.

"No, what's done is done. I don't give a rat's behind what anyone thinks." She patted Ivonne's shoulder. "And I don't mind telling you, after you left the study, I gave your Father a piece of my mind about this ridiculous marriage hullabaloo."

"I'm sorry you and Father quarreled." Ivonne sniffed as fresh tears threatened. "It's rather a mess, isn't it?"

Her mother opened her mouth then snapped it closed. She stared at Ivonne for a lengthy moment, uncertainty marring her expression.

"Have you considered ...? What I mean to say is, Ivonne is there the slightest possibility, that Mr. Faulkenhurst—"

"He's meeting with Lord and Lady Sethwick tonight regarding a position in America." Harder words Ivonne never spoke.

"Oh. I see." Mother wilted upon hearing the news. Nevertheless, she painted a brilliant smile onto her face. "We'll hatch a plan, darling. There's a little time, yet."

She didn't sound convinced by half. "Here, give me a hug, and then I must inform your father of our change in plans for this evening."

Ivonne pushed herself into a sitting position and shoved her hair out of her eyes.

"I'll check on you before I retire, dear." Mother embraced her, her familiar iris and jasmine perfume oddly comforting. With another reassuring smile, she slipped from the bedchamber.

The moment her mother exited the room, Ivonne collapsed against the pillows.

What was she to do? Falcon contemplated a move to America. Across the Atlantic. A lifetime away from her. She bit her lower lip and fiddled with the ribbon at her neckline.

The answer was simple.

She'd stow away on the ship.

14

"How much?" Chance ran a hand through his hair in disbelief.

Surely he'd heard wrong. There was some mistake. There had to be.

Fortune didn't smile on him. But perhaps God's favor finally had. He almost touched his jaw to make sure he wasn't gaping open-mouthed like a gasping mackerel.

"How much did you say?"

"Four hundred ninety-seven thousand pounds ... at last count." Mr. Belamont smiled kindly, his eyes twinkling. "It's rather a shock, I gather?"

"Yes, rather," Chance managed to utter, sounding almost normal. He was a wealthy man.

A very wealthy man. A virtual nabob.

In one wondrous moment he'd gone from nearly penniless soldier to prosperous investor. Most importantly, he now had the means to care for Ivy, which meant Viscount Wimpleton would welcome his request to marry her. Only last evening Chance had expressed his concerns to Allen regarding the matter, and today, that worry no longer existed.

"I kept your documents locked in a private cabinet Tobbins doesn't have access to. Given the amount of your fortune, I thought that wisest." Belamont slanted his silvery head toward the closed door. "He's efficient, but the man babbles when he's taken a nip or is nervous."

"Yes, I experienced that the other day." Chance attempted to calm his thundering pulse.

"All the information regarding Mr. Robinson's business ventures on your behalf are detailed here." Belamont pushed the documents across his desk for Chance's inspection. He pointed to the pages lined with neat columns of numbers. "It appears he invested heavily in silk and spices. Most wise."

Rubbing his injured hand, Chance stared at the ledger, noting row after row of scrupulous records. He met the solicitor's amused gaze. "I don't understand how you came to have this information."

Belamont relaxed into his chair, his hands folded across his slight paunch. "Robinson told me you gave him my name. When he couldn't reach you in India, he forwarded your correspondences to me."

Chance fingered the edge of the desk. Discovering one was wealthy did rather set one's nerves on edge. Not that he had any complaints, mind you. "I'd forgotten I'd told him you were my solicitor."

Overnight, everything fell into place in such a miraculous way; he couldn't believe his good fortune.

"I suggest you call on him today. You might as well deal directly with one another from this point onward." Sitting upright, Mr. Belamont withdrew a key from inside his coat. He unlocked a drawer then rummaged around a bit. "Where did I put that bank note?"

A triumphant smile lit his face. "Ah, here it is."

He removed the note before dutifully relocking the drawer and placing the key in his pocket. "This is yours. Robinson sent the funds last week, and I didn't have time to deposit the note before I left Town. By the way, Coutts & Company Bank is holding your monies."

Chance accepted the note, giving it a perfunctory glance. Another six thousand pounds plus change. He grinned unabashedly. "I'm not going to even attempt reserved composure. In fact, Belamont, count yourself fortunate that I'm not dancing you about the room."

"You've good reason to celebrate." Belamont released a gravelly chuckle. He swept his hand in a mocking bow. "Dance away, Faulkenhurst."

After folding the note, Chance tucked it into his pocket. He stood and gathered his possessions. Sobering, he faced the solicitor and extended his hand.

"Thank you for your diligence and honesty."

Mr. Belamont came around his desk. He gripped Chance's palm in a firm handshake. "It's been my pleasure to be of service. Tell me, if you don't mind, what's the first thing you're going to do with your newfound fortune?"

Chance clapped his beaver hat on his head and

grinned. "Buy a wedding ring."

Half an hour later, his mind still partially numb from pleasant shock, Chance inspected the rings the jeweler displayed for him. Primarily glittering diamonds, rubies, sapphires, and emeralds, he dismissed most with a cursory glance. Ivy deserved something unique, like her. He pictured glistening ivory-tinted pearls, the exact color of her skin as she lay naked atop their bed.

"Do you have anything less ostentatious? Something with pearls, perhaps? My intended prefers simplicity." At least he hoped to make her his intended before the day ended.

Ivy, his bride.

Indescribable elation sluiced through him.

"Yes, sir." The jeweler rummaged in the glass case.

"Ah, here we are." With great reverence, he produced a pearl and opal cluster ring. "This is a black opal, though if you'll notice, there's a strong blue color play."

Chance lifted the ring, holding it to the light

streaming in from the storefront window. A mazarine blue opal lay nestled amongst double rows of creamy seed pearls. Exquisite. "Have you any matching pieces?"

"Why, yes, there are." An excited glint entered the jeweler's eyes. He produced a grand parure set complete with earrings, necklace, pin, bracelet, and a delicate tiara.

"I'll take the entire set."

Ivy would be resplendent wearing them on their wedding day. For the first time, Chance harbored a genuine belief she'd be his bride.

God truly must be smiling down on him.

"Very good. Your lady is very fortunate indeed."

Chance shook his head. "No, I'm the one who's been blessed."

After locking the display case and securing the key inside his coat pocket, the jeweler gathered the gems. "Let me wrap them for you. I'll be but a moment."

"Thank you." Chance flipped his watch open. Less than an hour until his appointment with Lord Wimpleton. His stomach seized with unfamiliar nerves.

Steady on, old man.

He grinned. What a difference a single day could make in determining one's future. Belamont's missive early this morning, followed by a call to the solicitor, and then an appointment with Robinson had set a whole new course for Chance's life.

Now, the only tasks that remained were to win Lord Wimpleton's approval and to propose to Ivy.

"Miss Ivonne, you need to wake up."

Dawson's singsong greeting yanked Ivonne from a rather wonderful dream about a wedding. Her wedding.

"Your Father requests your presence below stairs," the maid said, followed by the sounds of her laying out Ivonne's morning tea.

Two days in a row? Seriously?

Ivonne flopped onto her back, her eyes firmly shut

as she tried to recall the man standing beside her at the altar of St. George's Parish Church.

No use, bother and blast.

His face flitted away on the fringes of her memory. And bother again. The one man she would ever accept as a groom decided to toddle off to the confounded colonies.

Her throat closed as a sudden rush of tears threatened. She clamped her lips together. No, by George, she wasn't casting her lot in that easily. She could at least ask Falcon to consider marrying her.

Then there'd be no doubt in her mind, lingering year upon incessant year. No always wondering if the outcome of her life might have been different if she'd only plucked up a feather's worth of courage and asked him if he would be her husband.

A cup rattled in a saucer near Ivonne's head. She opened one eye and sniffed.

Hot chocolate. Dawson's attempt at bribery.

"I brought you a cocoa topped with Devonshire cream." Dawson lowered the painted floral saucer to eye level. Thick rivulets of melted cream dripped over the teacup's rim. "You'd best take a sip. I was a mite too enthusiastic with the cream. I know you have a preference for it."

Dawson extended the cup and saucer, a hopeful expression on her face.

Poor dear.

She'd fussed and clucked so much last evening, Ivonne had finally snapped at the maid to leave her be. Immediately chagrined by her churlish behavior, Ivonne longed to apologize, but Dawson had taken her at her word and not returned to the chamber until this morning.

Ivonne sat up. She fluffed the pillows behind her back before accepting the hot chocolate. "Thank you, Dawson."

She took a sip and smiled. "Delicious."

The maid beamed, and after giving Ivonne a pat on the shoulder, set about selecting something appropriate for her to wear.

A full hour later, attired in a pink and white calico morning gown, she caught a glimpse of herself in a hallway mirror. At her request, Dawson had trimmed her hair before twisting the thick mass into a complex Grecian knot. Several curls framed Ivonne's face, softening her features.

She'd experimented with the new cosmetics Emmy sent too. Well-pleased with the effect, she smiled. The paints enhanced her features, although no one could tell she wore any. Just how many other ladies of her acquaintance availed themselves of the same devices and feigned natural beauty?

Once again, Ivonne stood outside Father's study, except today she had determined to take charge of her future. With a brisk knock, she thrust her chin upward a notch and pressed the latch, entering without waiting for permission.

She tripped to an abrupt stop.

Falcon, his legs crossed, lolled in an armchair across from her parents on the sofa.

Allen, one arm resting on the mantel, stood before the fireplace. His countenance remained unreadable, although a smile hovered about his mouth.

Why was Falcon here, closeted with her family? A quick perusal of their faces revealed nothing.

Allen strode to her and, after kissing her cheek, chucked her under the chin. "Courage, minx."

He turned to the others, now standing as well.

"I'm off to Tattersall's. Rumor has it Blackeridge has some prime bit of blood up for auction. I'll keep an eye out for a matched team for you, Falcon." With a smart salute, Allen departed the room.

"Darling, do have a seat." Her mother indicated the settee, as she moved toward the entrance. She paused and bussed Ivonne's cheek. Then, with a fervent hug, whispered, "All will be well, dearest."

What in the world?

Mother, too, made her escape, leaving Ivonne standing befuddled in the center of the study. Why did she need courage, and what would be well? First casting her father a questioning glance, she allowed her gaze to feast on Falcon.

No man should be that beautiful.

The black of his cutaway coat and the royal blue of his striped waistcoat made his eyes more vivid. How could his eyelashes be so dark with hair that fair?

His gaze leisurely roamed her length. Hot little

pricks of awareness popped out along the visual path his gaze traveled.

Gads.

Her senses came alive with strange little prickles as they were wont to do when he looked at her that way. If his eyes alone had the power to arouse her this much, imagine what his touch would do. She'd be sliding off her chair if he kept gazing at her so seductively.

She cleared her throat and focused on her father as she advanced further into the room. "Whatever is going on?"

"I think I'll let Faulkenhurst explain." He smiled and winked. After a quick embrace, Father strode from the room, leaving the door ajar.

Staring at the entry, Ivonne shook her head. "Is everyone dicked in the nob this morning?"

Falcon chuckled, that delicious rumble that sent her pulse skittering out of control. "No, they know we have something of importance to discuss and wished to give us some privacy."

Lord, no.

He's leaving for America. She wasn't prepared. It

was way too soon.

Her legs now the consistency of warm pudding, she wobbled to the sofa. Scrutinizing his dear face, she plopped ungracefully onto the cushion. She swallowed, fisting her hands in her skirt's folds. She couldn't bear his going away again.

"You're sailing to America. I hadn't thought you'd leave quite this soon." She tried to smile, but her lips refused to turn upward.

Falcon sat beside her. "Ivy, I'm—"

Palm outward, Ivonne raised her arm and cut him off. Her hand quivered so badly, she lowered it to her lap. She must propose this very minute, before he had a chance to say another word.

"Please, I have something to ask you, and if I don't ask now, I'll never have the courage again." She closed her eyes and sucked in a steadying breath. Squaring her shoulders, she opened her eyes and stared directly into the azure depths of his. "I don't suppose you'd consider...? That is, would you be opposed to...?"

Quivering from nervousness, Ivonne could barely

make her tongue work. She tried again despite her shaky voice. "I wanted to know if you would ...?"

Dash it all, this wasn't how she'd imagined the proposal would go. She lowered her eyelashes as the heat of humiliation crept steadily from her bosom to her cheeks. They likely glowed like candied apples as they did when she was embarrassed. Nonetheless, she must do this.

She peeped at him through her eyelashes.

A bemused expression on his face, Falcon stared at her. "Go on."

"Will you marry me?" she blurted in a breathy rush.

"Yes."

"I know I'm not ..." Her gaze jumped to meet his, and her heart hammered so hard, she could scarcely breathe. "Yes?"

The word emerged as a strangled squeak. She dared a tiny smile.

"You said yes? You'll marry me? Really?"

Falcon smiled, his perfect white teeth a stark contrast against his tanned face. He cupped her cheek with his good hand.

"Ivy, your father granted me permission to propose to you just moments ago."

Ivonne's mouth dropped open. "Oh."

Placing a finger beneath her chin, Falcon closed her mouth. His lips hitched upward into one of his irresistible smiles. "It seems he's been waiting for me to return to England and ask for your hand. I asked to marry you once before, and he refused."

"You did? *He did*?"

Father had turned Falcon away? How could he?

All these years she'd yearned for his love, and he'd already asked her father to marry her. Just wait until she had a moment alone with her sire. She'd give him a colorful earful he wouldn't soon forget.

"He wanted me to come back when you were older and I had the means to take care of you. However, your father realized you loved me, had been pining for me all these years."

Ivy angled her head proudly. "I wasn't pining."

"No?" Falcon quirked a brow.

She lifted a shoulder. "I just never entertained any

notion of marrying anyone else."

Eyeing the door, she suddenly stiffened, tucking her chin to her chest. "Father turned you away because you weren't wealthy? I never thought him so shallow."

"He wanted to make sure I loved you for you, and not your marriage settlement. He told me, just now, that when he realized I truly loved you and you loved me, he'd been waiting for me to return and ask for you again."

Chance ran a finger along her jaw.

"He loves you very much and only wants to see you happy."

He took her hand in his calloused one.

"I came here today seeking his permission to wed you. Your father summoned you so I could propose. Only you, minx," Falcon tapped the end of her nose, "beat me to it."

He'd been about to propose to her? Her heart soaring on wings of joy, she managed a tremulous smile.

Scooting nearer, he gathered her in his arms. "Though you were too young and I knew we'd have to wait, I've wanted to make you my bride since you were fifteen."

"Truly?" She blinked back tears of elation.

"I swear." His golden head descended until only an inch separated their lips. "I love you, Ivy. Will you be my bride?"

His mouth grazed hers, a tantalizing promise.

"Yes, Falcon, I shall." With a sigh, she sealed her promise with love's binding kiss.

Epilogue

London, England
Late June, 1818

Standing before the rector, Ivonne smiled into Falcon's loved-filled eyes.

They were married. She'd dreamed that this day might come. Seated in the front pew, resplendent in a plum cutaway coat and matching breeches trimmed with diamonds and rubies, the Prince Regent beamed his approval.

Falcon's family, as well as hers and Miss Kingsley, of course, completed the witnesses. Dozens of guests awaited them at home where an extravagant wedding breakfast had been prepared.

"I love you, Mrs. Faulkenhurst." Falcon caressed her palm with his thumb.

A delicious tremor shook her. What his touch did to her.

"And I love you."

"What say you we make our escape?" He grasped her hand and hurried her past the small crowd of laughing well-wishers to the waiting carriage.

Ivonne giggled when he tickled her ribs while lifting her into the conveyance.

"Ah, my wife is ticklish." After jumping into the vehicle, he promptly lowered the window coverings.

Settling her on his lap, he proceeded to nuzzle her neck and caress her ribs.

A new bout of giggles ended on a blissful sigh when Falcon claimed her lips in a scorching kiss. She leaned into him, surrendering to her desire, daring to meet his tongue with her own as she slipped her hands beneath his shirt. Hard muscles and warm flesh met her exploring fingers. She'd never tire of touching him.

Several tantalizing moments passed before Ivonne angled away from him. He needed to know she understood theirs wouldn't be the typical wedding night. But how to say so delicately was a bit of a pickle. It wouldn't do to offend Falcon on their wedding day.

"Falcon?"

"Why the serious face?" Bending his neck, he nibbled along her collarbone. He ventured ever lower, releasing her breasts from their confines. He gently cupped the mounds, raining kisses across the sensitive flesh.

God, she would die if he didn't take a nipple in his mouth.

As if he heard her thoughts, he encircled an aching tip with his warm lips. He suckled, grazing the end with his teeth.

A stab of intense pleasure flickered between her legs. She gasped and clutched his head, making him stop. She couldn't think straight when he kissed her so.

"This is important," she gasped, barely recognizing the husky voice as her own. "Please listen."

He raised his head, peering into her eyes.

"All right." He brushed a stray curl from her face.

"What is it you are determined to tell me, wife? I have other things I'd rather be doing than chatting."

He stared pointedly at her breasts before sweeping a finger across the top of the mounds. He dipped lower, softly scraping a fingernail across a turgid nipple.

She gasped again, unprepared for the hot desire flooding her. She seized his wandering finger and eyed him, afraid to say anything to disrupt his happiness.

"Come on, love. Out with it." He gave her a playful prod in the ribs.

Ivonne rested against his hard chest.

"You know I love you? No matter what?" She angled her head to peek at him.

His gorgeous mouth slid into one of his stunning smiles. "I know. And I love you. Tell me, what has you worried?"

"I don't mind that we cannot have children." She touched the scar on his cheek.

Falcon stilled and made an inarticulate sound in his throat. His eyes rounded, and his jaw sagged. He stared at her with such intensity, she squirmed on his lap and dropped her gaze to her hands.

He tilted her chin upward with a finger until their eyes met. "Pray tell me, why do you think we cannot have children?"

"Well, because you ..." Ivonne gazed at him warily. Her focus sank to his cravat as she whispered, "You lost your manhood in India."

He threw back his head, exposing the strong column of his throat and laughed, a rich unrestrained guffaw.

"Well, I certainly do not think it's a laughing matter," she huffed, nonplussed by his reaction.

His chest shaking from amusement, Falcon wiped at his eyes.

"Darling, let me assure you, my manhood is in perfect working order." He gripped her hips, holding her firmly to his lap, and shifted his hips upward.

Something hard flexed against her bottom.

"Oh. Oh! Is that your ...?"

"Indeed." He waggled his eyebrows, a wolfish grin on his mouth.

"It works properly?"

He pressed his rigid length against her buttocks once more. "Most assuredly, madam."

Melting into his arms, Ivonne sighed and raised her lips in invitation.

"Then everything is absolutely perfect."

About the Author

USA Today Bestselling, award-winning author COLLETTE CAMERON® scribbles Scottish and Regency historicals featuring dashing rogues and scoundrels and the intrepid damsels who re-form them. Blessed with an overactive and witty muse that won't stop whispering new romantic romps in her ear, she's lived in Oregon her entire life, though she dreams of living in Scotland part-time. A self-confessed Cadbury chocoholic, you'll always find a dash of inspiration and a pinch of humor in her sweet-to-spicy timeless romances®.

Explore **Collette's worlds** at
www.collettecameron.com!

Join her **VIP Reader Club** and **FREE newsletter**.
Giggles guaranteed!

FREE BOOK: Join Collette's The Regency Rose® VIP Reader Club to get updates on book releases, cover reveals, contests and giveaways she reserves exclusively for email and newsletter followers. Also, any deals, sales, or special promotions are offered to club members first. She will not share your name or email, nor will she spam you.

http://bit.ly/TheRegencyRoseGift

From the Desk of Collette Cameron

Dearest Reader,

I'm truly delighted you chose to read ***A Bride for a Rogue*** and hope it capitated you enough to take a peek at the other books in the series.

Ivonne and Chance's story was inspired by a scene in ***A Kiss for a Rogue***, the first book in my Honorable Rogues® series. My wounded hero needed a special heroine, and he found that in kindhearted Ivonne.

Please consider telling other readers why you enjoyed this book by reviewing it. Not only do I truly want to hear your thoughts, reviews are crucial for an author to succeed. **Even if you only leave a line or two, I'd very much appreciate it.**

So, with that I'll leave you.

Here's wishing you many happy hours of reading, more happily ever afters than you can possibly enjoy in a lifetime, and abundant blessings to you and your loved-ones.

Collette Cameron

A Rogue's Scandalous Wish

The Honorable Rogues®, Book Three

Formerly titled Her Scandalous Wish

A marriage offered out of obligation…
…an acceptance compelled by desperation.

At the urging of her dying brother, Philomena Pomfrett reluctantly agrees to attend a London Season. If she fails to acquire a husband, her future is perilous. Betrayed once by Bradford, Viscount Kingsley, as well as scarred from a horrific fire, Philomena entertains no notions of a love-match. Hers will be a marriage of convenience. *If* she can find man who will have her.

When the woman he loves dies, Bradford leaves England and its painful memories behind. After a three-year absence, he returns home but doesn't recognize his first love when he stumbles upon her hiding in a shadowy arbor during a ball. Something about the mysterious woman enthralls him, and he steals a moonlit kiss. Caught in the act by Philomena's brother, Bradford is issued an ultimatum—a duel or marry her.

Bradford refuses to duel with a gravely-ill man and offers marriage. But Philomena rejects his half-hearted proposal, convinced he'd grow to despise her when he sees her disfiguring scars. Then her brother collapses, and frantic to provide the medical care he needs, she's faced with marrying a man who deserted her once already.

Enjoy the first chapter of
A Rogue's Scandalous Wish
The Honorable Rogues®, Book Three

1

One, two, three, four ... No, I think there are actually five.

Yawning behind her partially open fan, Philomena peeked through the leaves of the enormous cage-shaped potted ficus and counted the wiry hairs sprouting from Lady Clutterbuck's chin. The chinwag and her cronies gossiped a short distance away, their unending litany contributing to the onset of Philomena's nagging headache.

She relaxed a fraction. No sign of Mr. Wrightly, a repugnant would-be suiter, and the reason she'd dove behind the plant when she spied him looking for her earlier.

Pressing two fingertips between her eyes to ease the thrumming there, she located the mantle clock and breathed out a soft sigh. Not yet ten o'clock. She allowed a droll smile. Giles wouldn't consider leaving before the supper dance.

No indeed.

Your brother is determined to find you a husband before Season's end, Philomena Martha Elizabeth Pomfrett. Whether you like it or not.

And she most emphatically did not.

Despite her lack of interest, or the cost to his already fragile health, dear Giles dutifully escorted her to event after event, evening after evening. And she obediently—well, more aptly, reluctantly—husband-hunted.

Content to become a spinster, the mercenary process conflicted with her principles and put her out of sorts, but Giles's time ran short so, for his sake, she pressed onward. Fear of her prospective husband's reaction to her scars created a permanent knot in her belly, and she swallowed against the dryness in her mouth.

Enough.

She shoved the worry aside. She'd deal with that obstacle when the time came. First she had to acquire a spouse, and her prospects weren't altogether promising.

"Oh, would you look at that delicious specimen of manhood." The lascivious tone of Lady Clutterbuck's cohort was entirely inappropriate for an aged, married peeress. "Utterly Scrumptious. Do you know who *he* is?"

The dame actually licked her lips, and thrust her bosoms skyward. Considering her breasts' monstrous size, they barely lifted above her ample waist, and a mere moment later, breathing heavily, she sagged into her former sack-shaped posture.

What unfortunate gentleman had found himself the target of the peeress's lewd attention *this* evening?

"Bradford, Viscount Kingsley. He's just come into his title. One hopes he proves himself worthy of the honor and avoids associating with inferiors and underlings." Lady Clutterbuck's strident voice plowed into Philomena with the force of a winter gale. The dame jutted her superior nose into the air. "That's become so common of late with all the mushrooms and nabobs thinking to force their way into Polite Society. Deep pockets are no substitute for good breeding, I say."

Bradford? Here?

Philomena craned her neck to see around the blasted plant.

Where?

Breath held, she deftly parted the foliage and bent forward.

There, at the ballroom's entrance in his formal evening attire, looking every bit the gentleman of refinement with his lovely auburn-headed sister, Olivia, on one arm and the distinguished Duchess of Daventry on the other. Unable to deny the giddiness seeing him again brought, fleeting excitement filled Philomena.

He swept the room with his brilliant, blue-eyed—slightly bored—gaze, and she jerked backward, kicking the container as she tumbled into the wall.

He can't see you, ninny.

A ROGUE'S SCANDALOUS WISH Excerpt

The gossips snapped curious, somewhat distracted glances in her direction.

Drat it all.

She dropped into a crouch with only her forehead visible above the blue and white porcelain, and in a moment, they put their graying heads together and launched into another round of *on dit*. For the first time, Philomena gave thanks that rumors dominated their narrow, peevish minds.

Peering between the ficus's woven branches, she bit her lip as her stomach toppled over itself. She wasn't ready to see Bradford. Face tanned, his raven hair glistening in the candlelight, he threw back his head and laughed at something the duchess said.

How could he have grown even more beautiful? Deucedly unfair to womanhood.

Still squatting, she pivoted right, and then shuffled left. Where was Giles? He'd promised her a beverage several minutes ago. He was nowhere to be seen, at least not from this awkward position.

Most likely, he'd gotten snared in a conversation with another hard-of-hearing matron. That's what came of exploiting their distant connection to the Dowager Marchioness Middleton in order to introduce Philomena to Polite Society.

Not one of the ladies in the dame's favored circle boasted a birthday less than five and seventy years ago, and inevitably, a matron or two or three, imposed upon him to fetch a ratafia, escort her to the card room, retrieve a wrap, or some other trivial matter. Kindhearted, Giles had never been able to politely make his excuses, so he amiably did as they bid.

Half the time, the old birds didn't need what they requested. They just enjoyed a handsome young man's attention for a few moments.

Biting her lower lip, Philomena braved another glance to the ballroom's entrance. Bradford had disappeared into the crowd as well.

Good. She could make her escape.

A cramp seized her calf as she moved to rise. Curses. Closing her eyes, she gripped the pot's edge, waiting for the spasm to pass. Pray God no one came upon her hugging the pottery. Rather hard to explain her sudden rapt interest in dirt and greeneries.

A ROGUE'S SCANDALOUS WISH Excerpt

Easing upright, she surreptitiously examined those nearest her. No one had noticed her. Pretty much a testament to her entire dismal Season. An incomparable, she was not.

Ah, here came Giles now, bearing a glass of ratafia in one hand and punch in the other. His limp had become more pronounced, and his countenance more wan, than it had been scarcely twenty minutes ago. Nonetheless, despite the ravages of ill-health, his striking visage turned many a fair maid's head as he ambled toward her hiding place.

Why did he insist on putting them through this every night?

He wants to make certain you are provided for when ...

She blinked away the familiar prickle of tears and the accompanying rush of anger. His delicate heart could fail at any moment. The injustice galled. He should be strong and healthy, seeking a spouse himself, not gravely weakened by a prolonged fever and resigned to an early death.

How she wished there'd been no need for him to

enlist, wished he hadn't been stationed in the West Indies, hadn't been wounded, had received proper treatment. Hadn't contracted Scarlet Fever.

If wishes were horses, beggars would ride.

Forcing composure, Philomena schooled her features into pleasant lines. She would bear her grief with quiet dignity.

His forehead furrowed, Giles peered about in search of her.

Eager to intercept him, and grateful to be spared overhearing more of Lady Clutterbuck's malicious claptrap, Philomena skirted the pot and, after edging along the wall a few feet, stepped out into the open.

Perhaps he would consider joining her in a game of loo or whist. His resting a spell at the card tables would also spare her another partnerless set or two. Blasted hard to acquire a husband when she spent most dances tapping her toes or pretending absorption in cornices, portraits, and elaborately painted ceiling panels.

"There you are." Passing her the ratafia, Giles grinned and winked, his gray-green eyes, so like hers, glinting with mirth. He dipped his honey-blond head near her ear. "Hiding again, little sister?"

He knew her too well.

She shook her head before taking a sip of the overly-sweet beverage. "No, I'm just avoiding—"

"Is that Kingsley?" Gaze as steely and cold as his tone, Giles canted his head to a cluster of guests not more than thirty feet away.

Philomena had thought Bradford attractive across the wide room, but this devilish, rake was garnering moon-eyed sighs and giggles from the younger misses and calculating, seductive glances from the faster, mature set. He hadn't seen her yet, and she wheeled around, presenting her back. The air clamped in her lungs so fiercely, her head spun dizzily, and her glass slipped from her hand. "Oh, dear God."

Her ragged gasp alerted Giles, and he seized her drink, preventing an embarrassing mishap or calling Bradford's attention to her.

Scorn sharpened the planes of his thin face as he scowled at Bradford. Quaffing his remaining punch, Giles then tossed back her ratafia before taking both cups in one hand and maneuvering her into the crowd. His gaze, simmering with sympathy, plucked at her self-control.

"Why don't we take a turn about the terrace, Phil? A bit of fresh air might help steady your nerves and allow you a few moments to compose yourself."

So that you don't make an utter cake of yourself.

She refused to peek over her shoulder, stiffening her spine until the taut muscles between her shoulder blades pinched.

Had the women fluttering their eyelashes and sending coquettish smiles Bradford's way any notion how ridiculous they looked? Scant difference lay between their brazen invitations and those of seasoned, dockside harlots. Not that Philomena blamed them. He'd matured into an arresting figure of a man, while she concealed hideous scars, necessitating a gown far from the first peak of fashion.

Jealousy dowsed with pain nipped her heart. Once upon a time, he had reserved that charming, sensual smile for her alone. Well, she'd convinced her naïve, younger self he had.

A ROGUE'S SCANDALOUS WISH Excerpt

"It's just there, through those French windows. You go along, and I'll be right out after I find Lady Middleton's misplaced shawl and put these down or find a servant to take them." Giles nodded in the doors' direction and half-lifted the glasses. "Earlier, I noticed a charming path through the gardens we might stroll."

And exhaust himself further? No. A secluded bench was a far better option.

Dragging her musings from Bradford, flashing his enigmatic smile at the tittering females, Philomena gave a short jerk of her head. "Yes, yes, fresh air and a stroll. An excellent notion."

Escape before the tears she swore she'd stopped shedding for him breached the damn of her resolve and surged down her cheeks. Why did seeing him hurt so awfully after all this time?

She should be over him. Wanted to be over him. Had thought she was until this miserable instant. Joy and anguish at seeing him again wrestled fiercely, each vying for supremacy.

Stupid, fickle heart.

Curling her gloved fingers into fists, and with determination in each step, she deftly navigated through the throng, her focus locked on her refuge—the lantern-lit garden. Perhaps, like a mythical tree nymph, she could disappear into the greeneries for the rest of the evening. Truth be known, no one but Giles would miss her.

Bradford hadn't sent a single letter, not one, the miserable wretch. And neither had he attempted to contact her or Giles after the fire that took Mama's and Papa's lives and nearly hers as well. A blaze that had destroyed their home and that Bradford's fiend of an uncle had started in the sanctuary—accidentally, he claimed, the lying bugger.

Day after day during the months of her convalescence, Philomena had hoped and prayed Bradford would come to see her or at least send word. Her love gave her strength, gave her the will to fight to live, helped her bear the anguish of her healing burns and the horrific loss of her parents and home.

By the time she left her sick-bed, she had relinquished any expectation of hearing from him again. Standing before her aunt's filmy dressing table mirror,

A ROGUE'S SCANDALOUS WISH Excerpt

Philomena cringed at the havoc the fire had wreaked on her arms and chest. Yet she possessed a measure of gratitude too, that except for a few minor burns on her shoulders and neck, the rest of her body had been spared. Taking her heart and her youthful love, scarred as viciously as her body, she'd tucked them away, determined never to endure pain that torturous again.

Bradford's shallow promises—that he'd love her until the end of time, that as soon as he was old enough, he'd ask for her hand, that he couldn't wait to marry her, that their difference in stations didn't matter—all lies. He hadn't wanted a maimed wife after the fire, and now that he held a title, he could choose a diamond of the first water for his viscountess.

Bitter knowledge to her injured pride and wounded soul.

"You knew you'd probably see him, Phil." Giles steered her further away from the salivating dames and the man who'd trampled her heart. He pressed her elbow. "It's the talk of London, his arriving in England on the cusp of his uncle's death. At least you were spared his company the better part of the Season. And you've suitors aplenty to choose from. Why, just this evening, Mr. Wrightly asked if he might court you."

"He did?"

How ghastly.

Double her age, the thrice-widowed, rich nabob made no secret he sought a young wife to beget an heir on. Coarse, vulgar, and perpetually reeking of rancid lard and sweat, Mr. Wrightly had finally deduced no lady of consequence would consider his suit, so he'd lowered his standards and now directed his attention to Philomena.

Lucky her. As if she were that desperate. Yet. "Please tell me you said no."

"Of course I didn't." Giles affected an insulted mien. "That's for you to decide, but you must make a decision by this Season's end. We haven't the funds to sponsor another."

Neither would he likely live that long.

A quartet of giggling misses, trailed by plain-faced Lady Victoria Southwark, staring longingly at Bradford, plowed across their path, scurrying toward the row of chairs to which he had escorted his sister. Obvious as fur on a frog what they schemed. Empty-headed chits.

"We've nearly used the whole of what Aunt Alice bequeathed us." Tense lines bracketing his mouth, Giles veered his attention from the women.

He wouldn't even permit himself interest in a woman, and sympathy welled at the unfairness of his plight. What a superb husband and father he would have made.

"I know, Giles, and I am trying. Truly."

Philomena compelled her stiff lips to smile. They'd exhausted their connections as well, and if it hadn't been for imposing upon Aunt Alice's distant relation to the Dowager Marchioness of Middleton, no door in London would have opened to them—the insignificant offspring of a second son and his equally unremarkable wife. "There are still a few weeks left in the Season. All is not yet lost."

Giles accompanied her toward the open French windows, lines of fatigue already deepening around his bleary eyes. "I'm not worried, Phil. You've caught the attention of several eligible men, and with your beauty and wit, I've no doubt you shall have multiple offers."

Bless him for his optimism, but blinded by brotherly love, he exaggerated her potential. At two and twenty, with a very modest dowry and a torso and arms riddled with scars, she wasn't sought after.

Her beaux consisted of an ancient, almost deaf baronet with a mouthful of rotting teeth, a former sea captain who yet retained a cargo hold's peculiar odor, a pimply-faced youth in line for an earldom, whose mother had towed him away by his ear upon finding him declaring himself to Philomena at a musicale last week, a banker so tight in the pocket he'd worn the exact same clothing every time she'd encountered him and was wont to stuff his pockets with food when he thought no one looked, a fourth son, without a farthing to his name and a propensity to ogle every bosom within ten feet, and now—*God bless my remarkable good fortune*—the widower, Mr. Wrightly.

Yes, they made a dandy selection to pick from. Why, Philomena was all aflutter, trying to determine which of the extraordinary gentlemen to set her cap for. However could she possibly choose between

A ROGUE'S SCANDALOUS WISH Excerpt

them?

But choose she must.

To ease Giles's fretting, she'd given her word she would marry, in spite of not wishing to ever enter that state, and they truly had exhausted most of their meager funds. Despite making economies, they'd only enough money to pay the rent and their expenses through July. To keep them from the poor house, and prevent him from seeking employment, she must wed. He was too weak, and sure as the rich guzzled champagne, acquiring a menial position would mean a speedier end for him.

If any one of her suitors didn't set her stomach to roiling worse than a pitching deck during a tempest, she would've said her vows tomorrow.

Squaring her shoulders, Philomena offered him what she hoped was a brave smile.

What needs done, gets done.

Hopefully, none of her admirers lurked outside, for she'd no wish to encounter them alone. She hadn't curbed her tendency to speak her mind, an attribute not favored by males, and she wasn't in a position to spurn anyone's attentions just yet.

Almost to the exit, she touched his arm. "I'll meet you outside, Giles, as soon as you are able. Who knows, I might stumble upon yet another potential husband upon the terrace."

And Lady Clutterbuck might cease gossiping, and snowflakes won't melt in hell.

Haggard lines creased Giles's eyes, and he gave her a firm nudge. "Miss Kingsley is looking this way. Hurry, Phil, go before she recognizes us."

A Kiss for a Rogue

The Honorable Rogues®, Book One

Formerly titled A Kiss for Miss Kingsley

**A lonely wallflower. A future viscount.
A second chance at love.**

Olivia Kingsley didn't expect to be swept off her feet and receive a marriage proposal two weeks into her first Season. However, one delicious dance with Allen Wimpleton, and her future is sealed. Or so she thinks until her eccentric father suddenly announces he's moving the family to the Caribbean for a year.

Terrified of losing Olivia, Allen begs her to elope, but she refuses. Distraught at her leaving, and unaware of her father's ill-health, Allen doubts her love and foolishly demands she choose—him or her father.

Heartbroken at his callousness, Olivia turns her back on their love. The year becomes three, enough time for her broken heart to heal, and after her father dies, she returns to England.

Coming face to face with Allen at a ball, she realizes she never purged him from her heart.

But can they overcome their pasts and old wounds to trust love again? Or has Allen found another in her absence?

To Capture a Rogue's Heart

The Honorable Rogues®, Book Four

Formerly titled To Tame a Scoundrel's Heart

He recruited her to help him find a wife…
…and discovered she was the perfect candidate.

Her betrothed cheated on her.
Katrina Needham intended to marry her beloved major and live happily-ever-after—until he's seen with another woman. Distraught, and needing a distraction, she agrees to assist the rugged, and dangerously handsome Captain Dominic St. Monté find a wife. So why does she find herself entertaining romantic notions about the privateer turned duke?

He believed he was illegitimate.
When Nic unexpectedly inherits a dukedom and the care of his young sisters, he reluctantly decides he must marry. Afterward, if his new duchess is willing, he hopes to return to the sea-faring life he craves part-time. If she doesn't agree, he'll have no choice but to give up the sea forever.

Will they forsake everything for each other?
Nic soon realizes Katrina possesses every characteristic he seeks in a duchess. The more time he spends with the vivacious beauty, the more enamored he becomes. Still, he cannot ask for her hand. Not only is she still officially promised to another, she has absolutely no interest in becoming a duchess, much less a privateer's wife.

Can Nic and Katrina relinquish their carefully planned futures and trust love to guide them?

The Rogue and the Wallflower

The Honorable Rogues®, Book Five

Formerly titled The Wallflower's Wicked Wager

He loved her beyond anything and everything—precisely why he must never marry her.

Love—sentimental drivel for weak, feckless fools.
Since an explosion ravaged Captain Morgan Le Draco's face and cost him his commission in the Royal Dragoons, he's fortified himself behind a rampart of cynicism and distrust. He's put aside all thoughts of marrying until he risks his life to save a drowning woman. At once, Morgan knows Shona's the balm for his tortured soul. But as a wealthy noblewoman, she's far above his humble station and can never be his.

Love—a treasured gift reserved for those beautiful of form and face.
Scorned and ridiculed most of her adult life, Shona Atterberry believes she's utterly undesirable and is reconciled to spinsterhood. She hides her spirited

temperament beneath a veneer of shyness. Despite how ill-suited they are, and innuendos that Captain Le Draco is a fortune-hunter, she cannot escape her growing fascination.

Two damaged souls searching for love.
Shona is goaded into placing a wicked wager. One that sets her upon a ruinous path and alienates the only man who might have ever loved her. Is true love enough to put their pasts behind them, to learn to trust, and to heal their wounded hearts.

The Earl and the Spinster

The Blue Rose Regency Romances:
The Culpepper Misses, Book One

Formerly titled Brooke: Wagers Gone Awry

**An angry earl. A desperate spinster.
A reckless wager.**

For five years, Brooke Culpepper has focused her energy on two things: keeping the struggling dairy farm that's her home operating and preventing her younger sister and cousins from starving. Then one day, a stern-faced stranger arrives at their doorstep and announces he's the dairy's new owner and plans on selling the farm. Though she's outraged, Brooke can't deny the Earl of Ravensdale makes her pulse race in the most disturbing way.

Heath is incensed to discover five women call the land he won at the gaming tables their home. He detests everything about the country and has no desire to own a smelly farm, even if one of the occupants is the most intelligent, entrancing woman he's ever met.

Desperate, pauper poor, and with nowhere to take her family, Brooke rashly proposes a wager. Heath's stakes? The farm. Hers? Her virtue. The land holds no interest for Heath, but he finds Brooke irresistible, and ignoring prudence as well as his sense of honor, he just as recklessly accepts her challenge.

In a winner-takes-all bet, will they both come to regret their impulsiveness, especially when love is at stake?

Excerpt

Enjoy the first chapter of
The Earl and the Spinster
The Blue Rose Regency Romances:
The Culpepper Misses, Book One

Even when most prudently considered,
and with the noblest of intentions, one who
wagers with chance oft finds oneself empty-handed.
~*Wisdom and Advice*
The Genteel Lady's Guide to Practical Living

1

Esherton Green,
Near Acton, Cheshire, England
Early April 1822

Was I born under an evil star or cursed from my first breath?

Brooke Culpepper suppressed the urge to shake her fist at the heavens and berate The Almighty aloud.

The devil boasted better luck than she. My God, now two *more* cows struggled to regain their strength?

She slid Richard Mabry, Esherton Green's steward-turned-overseer, a worried glance from beneath her lashes as she chewed her lower lip and paced before the unsatisfactory fire in the study's hearth. The soothing aroma of wood smoke, combined with linseed oil, old leather, and the faintest trace of Papa's pipe tobacco, bathed the room. The scents reminded her of happier times but did little to calm her frayed nerves.

Sensible gray woolen skirts swishing about her ankles, she whirled to make the return trip across the once-bright green and gold Axminster carpet, now so threadbare, the oak floor peeked through in numerous places. Her scuffed half-boots fared little better, and she hid a wince when the scrap of leather she'd used to cover the hole in her left sole this morning slipped loose again.

From his comfortable spot in a worn and faded wingback chair, Freddy, her aged Welsh corgi, observed her progress with soulful brown eyes, his

THE EARL AND THE SPINSTER Excerpt

muzzle propped on stubby paws. Two ancient tabbies lay curled so tightly together on the cracked leather sofa that determining where one ended and the other began was difficult.

What was she to do? Brooke clamped her lip harder and winced.

Should she venture to the barn to see the cows herself?

What good would that do? She knew little of doctoring cattle and so left the animals' care in Mr. Mabry's capable hands. Her strength lay in the financial administration of the dairy farm and her ability to stretch a shilling as thin as gossamer.

She cast a glance at the bay window and, despite the fire, rubbed her arms against the chill creeping along her spine. A frenzied wind whipped the lilac branches and scraped the rain-splattered panes. The tempest threatening since dawn had finally unleashed its full fury, and the fierce winds battering the house gave the day a peculiar, eerie feeling—as if portending something ominous.

At least Mabry and the other hands had managed

to get the cattle tucked away before the gale hit. The herd of fifty—no, sixty, counting the newborn calves—chewed their cud and weathered the storm inside the old, but sturdy, barns.

As she peered through the blurry pane, a shingle ripped loose from the farthest outbuilding—a retired stone dovecote. After the wind tossed the slat around for a few moments, the wood twirled to the ground, where it flipped end over end before wedging beneath a gangly shrub. Two more shingles hurled to the earth, this time from one of the barns.

Flimflam and goose-butt feathers.

Brooke tamped down a heavy sigh. Each structure on the estate, including the house, needed some sort of repair or replacement: roofs, shutters, stalls, floors, stairs, doors, siding...dozens of items required fixing, and she could seldom muster the funds to go about it properly.

"Another pair of cows struggling, you say, Mr. Mabry?"

Concern etched on his weathered features, Mabry wiped rain droplets from his face as water pooled at his muddy feet.

"Yes, Miss Brooke. The four calves born this mornin' fare well, but two of the cows, one a first-calf heifer, aren't standin' yet. And there's one weak from birthin' her calf yesterday." His troubled gaze strayed to the window. "Two more ladies are in labor. I best return to the barn. They seemed fine when I left, but I'd as soon be nearby."

Brooke nodded once. "Yes, we mustn't take any chances."

The herd had already been reduced to a minimum by disease and sales to make ends meet. She needed every shilling the cows' milk brought. Losing another, let alone two or three good breeders...

No, I won't think of it.

She stopped pacing and forced a cheerful smile. Nonetheless, from the skeptical look Mabry speedily masked, his thoughts ran parallel to hers—one reason she put her trust in the man. Honest and intelligent, he'd worked alongside her to restore the beleaguered herd and farm after Papa died. Their existence, their livelihood, everyone at Esherton's future depended on the estate flourishing once more.

"It's only been a few hours." *Almost nine, truth to tell.* Brooke scratched her temple. "Perhaps the ladies need a little more time to recover." *If they recovered.* "The calves are strong, aren't they?" *Please, God, they must be.* She held her breath, anticipating Mabry's response.

His countenance lightened and the merry sparkle returned to his eyes. "Aye, the mites are fine. Feedin' like they're hollow to their wee hooves."

Tension lessoned its ruthless grip, and hope peeked from beneath her vast mound of worries.

Six calves had been guaranteed in trade to her neighbor and fellow dairy farmer, Silas Huffington, for the grain and medicines he'd provided to see Esherton Green's herd through last winter. Brooke didn't have the means to pay him if the calves didn't survive—though the old reprobate had hinted he'd make her a deal of a much less respectable nature if she ran short of cattle with which to barter. Each pence she'd stashed away—groat by miserable groat, these past four years—lay in the hidden drawer of Papa's desk and must go to purchase a bull.

Wisdom had decreed replacing Old Buford two years ago but, short on funds, she'd waited until it was too late. His heart had stopped while he performed the duties expected of a breeding bull. Not the worst way to cock up one's toes...er, hooves, but she'd counted on him siring at least two-score calves this season and wagered everything on the calving this year and next. The poor brute had expired before he'd completed the job.

Her thoughts careened around inside her skull. Without a bull, she would lose everything.

My home, care of my sister and cousins, my reasons for existing.

She squared her shoulders, resolution strengthening her. She still retained the Culpepper sapphire parure set. If all else failed, she would pawn the jewelry. She'd planned on using the money from the gems' sale to bestow small marriage settlements on the girls. Still, pawning the set was a price worth paying to keep her family at Esherton Green, even if it meant that any chance of her sister and three cousins securing a decent match would evaporate faster than a dab of milk on a hot cook stove. Good standing and breeding meant little if one's fortune proved meaner than a churchyard beggar's.

"How's the big bull calf that came breech on Sunday?" Brooke tossed the question over her shoulder as she poked the fire and encouraged the blaze to burn hotter. After setting the tool aside, she faced the overseer.

"Greediest of the lot." Mabry laughed and slapped his thigh. "Quite the appetite he has, and friendly as our Freddy there. Likes his ears scratched too."

Brooke chuckled and ran her hand across Freddy's spine. The dog wiggled in excitement and stuck his rear legs straight out behind him, gazing at her in adoration. In his youth, he'd been an excellent cattle herder. Now he'd gone fat and arthritic, his sweet face gray to his eyebrows. On occasion, he still dashed after the cattle, the instinctive drive to herd deep in the marrow of his bones.

Another shudder shook her. Why was she so blasted cold today? She relented and placed a good-sized log atop the others. The feeble flames hissed and spat before greedily engulfing the new addition. Lord, she prayed she wasn't ailing. She simply couldn't afford to become ill.

A scratching at the door barely preceded the entrance of Duffen bearing a tea service. "Gotten to where a man cannot find a quiet corner to shut his eyes for a blink or two anymore."

Shuffling into the room, he yawned and revealed how few teeth remained in his mouth. One sock sagged around his ankle, his grizzled hair poked every which way, and his shirttail hung askew. Typical Duffen.

"Devil's day, it is." He scowled in the window's direction, his mouth pressed into a grim line. "Mark my words, trouble's afoot."

Not quite a butler, but certainly more than a simple retainer, the man, now hunched from age, had been a fixture at Esherton Green Brooke's entire life. He loved the place as much as, if not more than, she, and she couldn't afford to hire a servant to replace him. A light purse had forced Brooke to let the household staff go when Papa died. The cook, Mrs. Jennings, Duffen, and Flora, a maid-of-all-work, had stayed on. However, they received no salaries—only room and board.

The income from the dairy scarcely permitted Brooke to retain a few milkmaids and stable hands, yet not once had she heard a whispered complaint from anyone.

Everybody, including Brooke, her sister, Brette, and their cousins—Blythe, and the twins, Blaike and Blaire—did their part to keep the farm operating at a profit. A meager profit, particularly as, for the past five years, Esherton Green's legal heir, Sheridan Gainsborough, had received half the proceeds. In return, he permitted Brooke and the girls to reside there. He'd also been appointed their guardian. But, from his silence and failure to visit the farm, he seemed perfectly content to let her carry on as provider and caretaker.

"Ridiculous law. Only the next male in line can inherit," she muttered.

Especially when he proved a disinterested bore. Papa had thought so too, but the choice hadn't been his to make. If only she could keep the funds she sent to Sheridan each quarter, Brooke could make something of Esherton and secure her sister and cousins' futures too.

If wishes were gold pieces, I'd be rich indeed.

Brooke sneezed then sneezed again. Dash it all. A cold?

The fresh log snapped loudly, and Brooke started. The blaze's heat had failed to warm her opinion of her second cousin. She hadn't met him and lacked a personal notion of his character, but Papa had hinted that Sheridan was a scallywag and possessed unsavory habits.

A greedy sot, too.

The one time her quarterly remittance had been late, because Brooke had taken a tumble and broken her arm, he'd written a disagreeable letter demanding his money.

His money, indeed.

Sheridan had threatened to sell Esherton Green's acreage and turn her and the foursome onto the street if she ever delayed payment again.

A ruckus beyond the entrance announced the girls' arrival. Laughing and chatting, the blond quartet billowed into the room. Their gowns, several seasons out of fashion, in no way detracted from their charm, and pride swelled in Brooke's heart. Lovely, both in countenance and disposition, and the dears worked hard too.

"Duffen says we're to have tea in here today." Attired in a Pomona green gown too short for her tall frame, Blaike plopped on to the sofa. Her twin, Blaire, wearing a similar dress in dark rose and equally inadequate in length, flopped beside her.

Each girl scooped a drowsy cat into her lap. The cats' wiry whiskers twitched, and they blinked their sleepy amber eyes a few times before closing them once more as the low rumble of contented purrs filled the room.

"Yes, I didn't think we needed to light a fire in the drawing room when this one will suffice." As things stood, too little coal and seasoned firewood remained to see them comfortably until summer.

Brette sailed across the study, her slate-blue

gingham dress the only one of the quartet's fashionably long enough. Repeated laundering had turned the garment a peculiar greenish color, much like tarnished copper. She looped her arm through Brooke's.

"Look, dearest." Brette pointed to the tray. "I splurged and made a half-batch of shortbread biscuits. It's been so long since we've indulged, and today is your birthday. To celebrate, I insisted on fresh tea leaves as well."

Brooke would have preferred to ignore the day.

Three and twenty.

On the shelf. Past her prime. Long in the tooth. Spinster. *Old maid.*

She'd relinquished her one chance at love. In order to nurse her ailing father and assume the care of her young sister and three orphaned cousins, she'd refused Humphrey Benbridge's proposal. She couldn't have put her happiness before their welfare and deserted them when they needed her most. Who would've cared for them if she hadn't?

No one.

Mr. Benbridge controlled the purse strings, and

Humphrey had neither offered nor been in a position to take on their care. Devastated, or so he'd claimed, he'd departed to the continent five years ago.

She'd not seen him since.

Nonetheless, his sister, Josephina, remained a friend and occasionally remarked on Humphrey's travels abroad. Burying the pieces of her broken heart beneath hard work and devotion to her family, Brooke had rolled up her sleeves and plunged into her forced role as breadwinner, determined that sacrificing her love not be in vain.

Yes, it grieved her that she wouldn't experience a man's passion or bear children, but to wallow in doldrums was a waste of energy and emotion. Instead, she focused on building a future for her sister and cousins—so they might have what she never would—and allowed her dreams to fade into obscurity.

"Happy birthday." Brette squeezed her hand.

Brooke offered her sister a rueful half-smile. "Ah, I'd hoped you'd forgotten."

"Don't be silly, Brooke. We couldn't forget your special day." Twenty-year-old Blythe—standing with her hands behind her—grinned and pulled a small, neatly-wrapped gift tied with a cheerful yellow ribbon from behind her. Sweet dear. She'd used the trimming from her gown to adorn the package.

"Hmph. Need seedcake an' champagne to celebrate a birthday properly." The contents of the tray rattled and clanked when Duffen scuffed his way to the table between the sofa and chairs. After depositing the tea service, he lifted a letter from the surface. Tea dripped from one stained corner. "This arrived for you yesterday, Miss Brooke. I forgot where I'd put it until just now."

If I can read it with the ink running to London and back.

He shook the letter, oblivious to the tawny droplets spraying every which way.

Mabry raised a bushy gray eyebrow, and the twins hid giggles by concealing their faces in the cat's striped coats.

Brette set about pouring the tea, although her lips twitched suspiciously.

Freddy sat on his haunches and barked, his button

eyes fixed on the paper, evidently mistaking it for a tasty morsel he would've liked to sample. He licked his chops, a testament to his waning eyesight.

"Thank you, Duffen." Brooke took the letter by one soggy corner. Holding it gingerly, she flipped it over. No return address.

"Aren't you going to read it?" Blythe set the gift on the table before settling on the sofa and smoothing her skirt. They didn't get a whole lot of post at Esherton. Truth be known, this was the first letter in months. Blythe's gaze roved to the other girls and the equally eager expressions on their faces. "We're on pins and needles," she quipped, fluttering her hands and winking.

Brooke smiled and cracked the brownish wax seal with her fingernail. Their lives had become rather monotonous, so much so that a simple, *soggy*, correspondence sent the girls into a dither of anticipation.

My Dearest Cousin...

Brooke glanced up. "It's from Sheridan.

Printed in Great Britain
by Amazon